HENRY JAG...

EATING

A Very Serious Comedy About Women & Food

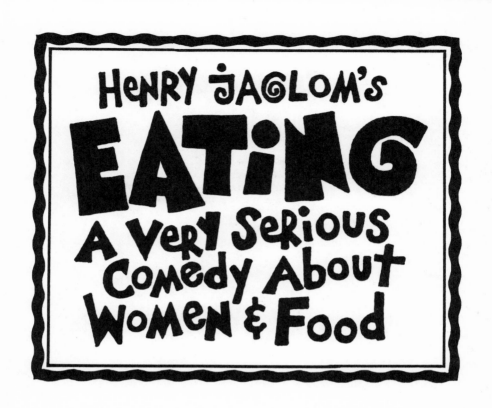

Henry Jaglom's EATING

A Very Serious Comedy About Women & Food

RAINBOW FILMBOOKS / SAMUEL FRENCH TRADE

HOLLYWOOD

ISBN 1-878965-01-8
LC 90-063561

Cover design by Heidi Frieder

Printed and bound in the United States of America

A Rainbow Filmbook
Distributed by
Samuel French Trade
7623 Sunset Blvd.
Hollywood, CA 90046

For My Mother, Marie

Contents

THE SCRIPT

EATING

MARTINE SETS UP A VIDEOCAMERA,
TELLING HERSELF, IN FRENCH, THAT IT IS NOW HER TURN.
SHE SITS DOWN FACING THE CAMERA AND SPEAKS INTO IT.

MARTINE : *Now tell me, do you have any problem*
about food? . . . God, I feel uncomfortable . . .
This is not easy stuff . . . Well, I think, I really
think I'm out of it now. But I've been through
a lot of it. And I still don't understand
completely why. And I think I'm always scared
that it could happen to me again. And until
I really have the feeling that I have the answers,
I will never feel safe, because I will always think
that it can happen again. And I think that's
why I'm doing all this stuff. To find out why . . .
Why it happened to me . . .

THE VIDEOCAMERA SLOWLY TURNS FROM MARTINE
TO FACE THE AUDIENCE.

TITLES.

HELENE IS IN HER KITCHEN, TURNING TAROT CARDS.
LYDIA, HER STEPDAUGHTER, ENTERS, CARRYING A RABBIT.

LYDIA : Hi, Chips. (She kisses her)

HELENE : Good morning. (She laughs) God, I told you
not to bring that rabbit in the house. She's got
rabbit fur all over me. Aren't you going to wish
me happy birthday?

LYDIA : Oh, happy birthday. (She kisses her again)

HELENE   : Thank you.

LYDIA   : (Looking at tarot cards) What've you got?

HELENE   : Well, I don't know. The Ace of One's upside down, let me check it out, it's not very good . . . I wanted something good today . . . Let's see. (She reads) "Take stock . . . Have a second look. Don't give up . . . Just try again . . . Lack of initiative, simply not trying . . ."

LYDIA   : That's not you.

HELENE   : (Reading) " . . . May be necessary to delay or temporarily cancel plans. No need to be depressed . . . "

LYDIA   : No need to be depressed!

HELENE   : No need to be depressed.

MARTINE ENTERS THE KITCHEN, IN HER NIGHTGOWN.

MARTINE   : Hello.

HELENE   : *Bonjour, Bonjour.*

MARTINE   : Happy birthday. (She kisses Helene)

HELENE   : Thank you.

MARTINE   : What are you *doing*?

HELENE   : (Continuing to read from book) "Clinging to old goals will prevent you from accepting new and wonderful opportunities."

MARTINE   : What are you doing?

HELENE	: I don't know, it doesn't sound so great. I don't want to release my old goals . . . I'm doing the *Tarot*, I'm trying to see what's coming up for the year.
MARTINE	: And so?
HELENE	: And so — "Being timid will only emphasize your weakness. Take the bull by the horns." (She turns to Lydia) Does your father run away on birthdays often?
LYDIA	: I love you, Chips. (She kisses her)
HELENE	: Yeah.
LYDIA	: I'm going to go do my exercises.
HELENE	: Yeah, do your exercises. (Lydia exits)
MARTINE	: Do you believe in these things?
HELENE	: Well, you know, I really do, actually. I do believe that something comes down from the universe . . .
MARTINE	: So, what do you have to do? *"Take the bull by horns?"*
HELENE	: (Laughs) I have to take the bull by the horns, yes.

EXTERIOR OF A SUBURBAN STREET.
KATE WALKS TOWARD HELENE'S HOUSE.

EXTERIOR POOL.
LYDIA DOES BALLET EXERCISES IN THE WATER, GRACEFULLY.

LATER: HELENE IS ALONE IN THE KITCHEN. THE PHONE RINGS.

HELENE   : Hello? Hi. Oh, thank you . . . Yeah, I'm very
            happy. I wish *you* were here . . . The party is
            going to be over around six. Okay? I think all
            the women'll be gone probably 6:30, 7. It'll be
            just you and me, babe. You ready for that?
            After all these years? "Still ready after all these
            years . . ." I love you, too. I love you a lot . . .
            Okay. 7 o'clock. On the dot!

EXTERIOR OF HELENE'S HOUSE.
HELENE HAS COME OUTSIDE TO PICK UP SUNDAY NEWSPAPER.
KATE WALKS UP THE STEPS TO THE ENTRANCE.

KATE   : Happy birthday! (They kiss)

HELENE   : Oh, Kate, I'm so glad you're here. Nobody
            else is here.

KATE   : Great.

HELENE   : And I'm going crazy because Naomi is not
            here yet.

KATE   : So what can I do to help?

HELENE   : I don't know what to wear. Will you help me
            decide?

KATE   : Sure.

HELENE   : Sadie's having her 50th, so I invited her to join us.

KATE   : Well, you couldn't have had a more perfect day.

THEY GO UP THE STAIRS TO HELENE'S BEDROOM.

HELENE	: What are *you* going to wear?
KATE	: I don't know. I brought this frilly thing. It's sort of strange, but what the hell, why not today.
HELENE	: I'm glad you're here. I'm glad we're sharing this day together. (Carrying the present that Kate has brought her) This is so pretty, I really love it.
KATE	: So show me what you've got.
HELENE	: Okay. Just wait right there. (She runs into her dressing room)
KATE	: (Pulls her own dress out of a bag) See, this is what *I* got, I don't know . . .

THE LIVING ROOM. LYDIA ENTERS WITH FOUR YOUNG WOMEN.
THEY ARE CARRYING FLOWERS AND OTHER DECORATIONS.

LYDIA	: (Mimicking adults) "I just don't like this decor, at *all*. No, no, *no*. These dead plants just do not *do* it, no, no, *no* . . ."

THE YOUNG WOMEN LAUGH, AS THEY START
TO DECORATE FOR THE PARTY.

HELENE'S BEDROOM.

HELENE	: Now, I have all sorts of things here that I *think* I can squeeze myself into.

THE FRONT DOOR. SOPHIE ENTERS, LOOKS AROUND.

SOPHIE	: Hello? *Hello?*

HELENE'S BEDROOM.

HELENE   : I just got this.

KATE   : Oh God, I love this material, it's so yummy.

HELENE   : Isn't it gorgeous? And the black is very
                slimming.

KATE   : No. Uh-uh . . .

HELENE   : No?

THE FRONT DOOR. SOPHIE IS STILL LOOKING AROUND.

SOPHIE   : *Helene?* (There is no answer. She exits into
                another part of the house)

HELENE'S BEDROOM.

HELENE   : This is lovely, too. I think the material is very
                flattering.

KATE   : Oh, I like that.

HELENE   : But the blue is very sexy. (Laughs) I mean, I
                don't know, it's really not quite *me*, but it, no, it
                zips up the front. See, it's short in the front.

KATE   : It's pretty Hollywood, isn't it?

HELENE   : It's a little Hollywood. (Laughs)

THE LIVING ROOM. THE YOUNG WOMEN ARE DECORATING,
PUTTING UP "HAPPY BIRTHDAY" THINGS AND TALKING.
OUT OF THE WINDOW, WE — AND THEY — SEE
MARTINE SUNBATHING, IN THE NUDE.

JEANIE   : Oh, *who* is that? . . . Lydia? . . .

LYDIA (V.O.)	:	What?
JEANIE	:	There's like this naked girl by your pool.
LYDIA (V.O.)	:	I know.
JEANIE	:	Who *is* she?
LYDIA (V.O.)	:	A guest.
JEANIE	:	Come *on*.
LYDIA (V.O.)	:	Her name's *Martine*.

OUTSIDE, BY THE POOL. SOPHIE IS SITTING AT A TABLE.

SOPHIE : Martine, come on over here! *Viens ici!* Come on, I want to see you . . . I 've had a horrible morning . . .

THE LIVING ROOM. THE YOUNG WOMEN STILL DECORATING.

HELENE'S BEDROOM. SHE IS OPENING KATE'S GIFT.

KATE : This is a *crystal* that I want you to meditate with.

HELENE : Oh, that's beautiful.

KATE : It seems to help a lot when you're stressed. And the *sage* . . . If you get crazy, and you burn it, it's supposed to get rid of all the negative energy. The Indians use it . . .

OUTSIDE, BY THE POOL. MARTINE JOINS SOPHIE.

SOPHIE : *Ça va?*

MARTINE : *Ça va bien!*

SOPHIE   : You look fantastic.

MARTINE   : (Laughs) Thank you.

SOPHIE   : You're going to drive all these women *crazy* today.

MARTINE   : Are they coming in right now? Do you think I should get dressed already?

SOPHIE   : No. Drive them nuts. Why is it that every woman who's French has a fantastic body?

MARTINE   : Oh, I don't think I have a fantastic body at all. I don't think in France a woman would come to another woman and tell her, "Well, you've got a fantastic body." It's amazing!

SOPHIE   : Yes, but they'd think it. But they wouldn't say it.

HELENE'S BEDROOM.

KATE   : Where's Frank?

HELENE   : Oh, he's in San Francisco. He's at a conference.

KATE   : What the hell is he doing there on your birthday?

HELENE   : Well, he's coming back. He's coming back tonight.

KATE   : Well, at least you get him tonight.

HELENE   : Yeah . . . So how can I lose? A lucky horseshoe, a crystal, a sage — (She laughs) — you've got me covered.

OUTSIDE, BY THE POOL.

SOPHIE   : I've been worried sick about Helene.

MARTINE   : Worried about Helene? Why?

SOPHIE   : Well, she's gotten fat. I think she's gained ten
                  pounds.

MARTINE   : You're crazy. She's not fat. She's just perfect.

SOPHIE   : No, she's gained weight. And she only gains
                  weight when she's really upset.

THE LIVING ROOM. THE YOUNG WOMEN DECORATING.

OUTSIDE, BY THE POOL.
KATE ENTERS, JOINS SOPHIE AND MARTINE.

KATE   : Hi.

SOPHIE   : Hi, sweetheart. Happy birthday. (They kiss)

KATE   : Oh. Thank you.

MARTINE   : Happy birthday? It's *your* birthday? (She
                  kisses her) I thought it was *Helene's* birthday.

SOPHIE   : No, it's *both* of their birthdays.

KATE   : The big 3-0.

MARTINE   : Oh. Happy birthday.

SOPHIE   : (To Kate) You've got a perm . . . I was telling
                  Martine that I was *very* worried about Helene.
                  I mean it's her 40th birthday, my God she's
                  so brave. Can you imagine, she's giving a party
                  for her 40th birthday? She's announcing to
                  everyone that she's 40 years old? I mean
                  I wouldn't even tell anyone I was *thirty*!
                  (She laughs and so do they)

THE LIVING ROOM. THE YOUNG WOMEN DECORATING.

THE STAIRCASE. SOPHIE IS COMING UP THE STAIRS TO
HELENE'S BEDROOM. HELENE IS LYING ON HER BED IN
THE BLUE "HOLLYWOOD" OUTFIT, EATING A MUFFIN.

SOPHIE   : Hello? Darling? Where's the birthday girl? . . .
                  Where are you? . . . Hi . . . Happy birthday . . .
                  What *is* that outfit? You're not going to wear
                  that are you? . . . We're 40 today, not 14.
                  Let's not forget that . . . You want to go downstairs?

HELENE   : No, I'm not going down.

SOPHIE   : Why?

HELENE   : I'm just not going.

SOPHIE   : Come on. Come downstairs with me.

HELENE   : No, I want to stay up here.

SOPHIE   : Helene?

HELENE   : Yes?

SOPHIE   : Come on.

HELENE   : Sophie . . .

SOPHIE   : It's your *birth*day. What's wrong with you?

HELENE   : I'm sitting here and I'm eating my muffin
                    and I'm having a delicious time . . . I can do
                    anything I want today, because it's my birthday,
                    and I can eat everything I choose . . .

SOPHIE   : Well, *I'm* going down. I'm going to have a
                    good time today whether you want to or not.

SOPHIE EXITS DOWN THE STAIRS.

HELENE STAYS ON HER BED, EATING THE MUFFIN.

THE KITCHEN.
TWO COOKS ENTER AND BEGIN SETTING UP FOR THE PARTY.
THE HEAD COOK IS NAOMI. HER ASSISTANT IS CONNIE.

NAOMI   : Just familiarize yourself with the kitchen,
                    okay?

CONNIE   : Where are the towels?

NAOMI   : They're in there, in the corner of the drawer
                    over there.

CONNIE   : Okay.

OUTSIDE BY THE POOL.
KATE AND MARTINE ARE ALONE NOW.

MARTINE   : So, how does it feel to turn 30?

KATE   : I don't really know yet.

MARTINE   : Well, it's going to happen to me very soon, so
                    I want to know.

KATE   : I hope you like it better than I do.

MARTINE   : Really?

KATE   : It's a little weird right now.

THE KITCHEN. HELENE ENTERS WEARING THE TOP OF ONE
DRESS, THE SKIRT OF ANOTHER UNDERNEATH.

HELENE   : Oh, Naomi, I'm so glad you're here. I was so
                worried.

NAOMI   : (Kisses her) Happy birthday.

HELENE   : Thank you.

NAOMI   : This is the big one, huh?

HELENE   : Yes. (To second cook) Hi.

NAOMI INTRODUCES CONNIE.
HELENE IS WORRIED ABOUT HER DRESS.

HELENE   : Do you like this? Do you think this is good?

NAOMI   : It's not my favorite.

OUTSIDE BY THE POOL. CLOSE UP OF KATE'S T-SHIRT.
IT SAYS: "I CAN'T BELIEVE I FORGOT TO HAVE CHILDREN."

MARTINE   : Did you really forget?

KATE   : Well, I have so far. I don't know, kids are . . .
                I think I have to grow up before I can deal
                with kids.

MARTINE   : Yes, that's also what I thought.

KATE   : It's a little overwhelming.   I mean at this point, that's like a commitment for ever and ever and ever, a man and kids . . . I find that terrifying.

MARTINE   : *You* have the man to *do* them with, don't you?

KATE   : Yeah. Yeah, I have a really good man.

MARTINE   : Well, that's a good start.

KATE   : Yeah. He's a good start.

THE FRONT DOOR. A KNOCK. HELENE RUNS TO ANSWER. IT IS SADIE, WHOSE 50TH BIRTHDAY IT IS.

SADIE   : Oh, happy birthday!

HELENE   : Happy birthday to *you*! (They kiss)

SADIE   : I love it . . . isn't it depressing?

OUTSIDE, BY THE POOL.

MARTINE   : I always thought when I was 30 it would be perfect, you know? I would reach my perfect age. I am very close to it now and it doesn't seem any better.

KATE   : I wish you luck.

MARTINE   : Thank you.

KATE   : I hope you're closer to it than me.

MARTINE   : Well, you seem very close to it to me. You
                 are happily married, aren't you?

KATE   : Yes. Very happily married . . .
                 It's — it's not always that simple. I still have
                 questions and doubts . . . Even though he's the
                 most wonderful man in the world.

HELENE'S BEDROOM.
HELENE IS GETTING DRESSED AGAIN, SADIE WATCHING.

HELENE   : (Looking in her mirror) I don't know. I'd like
                 something sort of low, but my neck . . . you
                 know . . . all these veins . . .

SADIE   : Oh God, you look like a baby to me. I wish I
                 was being 40 today.

HELENE   : Oh Sadie, you're so sweet.

SADIE   : And look at that, your hair looks like wheat
                 and straw in the sunlight there, the way the
                 light is hitting you . . . I'm so depressed.

HELENE   : *You're* so depressed?

SADIE   : Oh God, honey, I just hate turning 50. I just
                 hate this getting old. I just hate having to stay
                 thin so it'll make me feel young and maybe I
                 might get a man if my body's nice.

HELENE   : You know, we all have to love ourselves,
                 Sadie, we just do.

SADIE   : I hate that my tits are sagging!

OUTSIDE BY THE POOL.

MARTINE : I think you never stop questioning, you know? You always have doubts, whatever you choose.

KATE : Sometimes I just think that maybe I just want to screw it all up, you know? For fun, or something . . .

THE LIVING ROOM. THE YOUNG WOMEN ARE DECORATING. HELENE RUNS IN, STILL UNSURE WHAT TO WEAR.

HELENE : Lydia, I want you to look at *this* one. Look at this color.

YOUNG GIRL : Black.

HELENE : You like the black? I sort of like this one. You like the black better?

2ND GIRL : I like the gold.

3RD GIRL : I like the gold, too.

HELENE : Lydia, don't you think the black is more slimming?

MRS. WILLIAMS, HELENE'S MOTHER, ENTERS.

HELENE : (Surprised) *Mother*? (She runs to her) What are you *doing* here? I didn't know you were back in town. (They kiss)

MRS. WILLIAMS : Well, I wanted to surprise you. I had to come by and wish you happy birthday.

HELENE   : Well, you *did* surprise me.

MRS. WILLIAMS : I'm really so sorry. I ordered something really
                  special for you and it just hasn't come yet . . .
                  But you'll like it, I think.

HELENE   : Well, what is it?

MRS. WILLIAMS : It wouldn't be a surprise if I told you what it
                  is . . . I didn't know you were having a party.

HELENE   : Well, I'm just having a few friends over. Kate
                  and Sadie and *their* friends and just sort of
                  wishing each of us into a new decade.

MRS. WILLIAMS : Oh good. Well now, you have a good time.
                  Go back to your friends and I'll —

HELENE   : Oh, mother, no, no, no . . . I want you to stay.

MRS. WILLIAMS : Well, I told Sue I would drop by. You know
                  she's been —

HELENE   : Call Sue, I'll call Sue. Please stay, hmm?

OUTSIDE. A TABLE IN THE GARDEN.
SOPHIE AND KATE SIT ACROSS FROM ONE ANOTHER.

SOPHIE   : I mean, you've got it *all*. You've got this
                  fabulous husband who just *worships* you and
                  who's totally special and amazing with women
                  and open to everyone. I mean, here we are,
                  the rest of us, we're just absolutely in this
                  hopeless position with men. And you've just
                  got the whole package. Do you know how
                  lucky you are about your marriage?

THE LIVING ROOM. THE WOMEN ARE RESTING,
CHATTING, LAUGHING. MARTINE ENTERS.
SHE CARRIES HER VIDEOCAMERA IN A BAG.

JEANIE   : You have a *great* body!

MARTINE   : (She laughs and sits down) Well, thank you.

THE GARDEN TABLE.

SOPHIE   : I don't know . . . I don't know . . . Twelve
                    years? I don't think I could be with someone
                    for twelve years. I don't think I could take it.
                    I just have to move on after about a year and a
                    half. (She laughs; Kate smiles with her)

THE LIVING ROOM.

JEANIE   : Do you make films or something?

MARTINE   : Yes, I'm doing a documentary here. A film
                    documentary about California.

LYDIA   : On "L.A. people," you know.

JEANIE   : Do you do it without your top on, all the
                    time?

MARTINE   : (Laughing) No . . .

JEANIE   : *I* would do it if I could.

LONNIE   : She's the first topless filmmaker from France.

MARTINE   : Actually, would you mind answering some of
                    my questions, on camera? (She starts to unpack
                    the videocamera)

JEANIE : Why are you doing this? For what?

MARTINE : Well I'm doing it for French television, you know?

JEANIE : French *television?*

MARTINE : Yes. About Southern Californian behavior.

LYDIA : "Behavior." We sound like poodles.

MARTINE : You can talk about everything you are interested in.

LYDIA : It's going to be sent out in one of those space capsules, you know, to tell the world what L.A. people are like.

MARTINE : What are you *really* interested in?

LONNIE : I want to know when we're going to *eat*!

THE DEN, BY THE FIREPLACE.
SADIE IS TALKING WITH HELENE.

SADIE : I've been having this affair with this younger guy. I mean, he's 34 years old. You know, when he was six, I was in college . . .

HELENE : (Laughs) Sadie . . .

SADIE : . . . And I see the way he looks at Jennifer and I get jealous. And I try to hold it all in and I feel like I'm going to burst. I feel like I'm going to die and I think, I'll eat something, and I think, oh my God, if I eat something I'm going to get fat and if I get fat, then he won't want to be with an old broad like me.

THE LIVING ROOM. MARTINE HAS SET UP THE VIDEOCAMERA
AND IS INTERVIEWING ONE OF THE YOUNG WOMEN, LONNIE.

LONNIE : I feel hungry. I want something to eat.
I want to know what we're going to have. I'm
just starving. (She laughs)

MARTINE : Well, tell me, do you have — have you ever
had any diets? I mean have you been on diets?

LONNIE : I've been on every diet on the planet. And
right now I'm on the "I'm Allergic To Everything
On The Planet Diet."

THE KITCHEN. THE PHONE RINGS AND HELENE RUSHES IN
TO ANSWER IT.

HELENE : Hello? Frank? Hi! Listen, I'm just — I'm just
in the middle of everything . . . You know,
mother came . . .

THE LIVING ROOM. LONNIE IS CONTINUING HER
INTERVIEW. NOW SHE IS TALKING INTO MARTINE'S
CAMERA, DIRECTLY AT US.

LONNIE : *I used to like to sit in front of the TV with a big
bowl of oatmeal and just sit there with a bunch
of brown sugar watching television, and just eat.
I just liked to eat all of the time. And somehow it
made me feel like I was full inside, because it
was so empty when I wasn't eating. It was just
like there was this big black hole in space that
was inside of me that nothing could ever fill . . .
I was just depressed at five. But there was this
candy store right down the street from where I
lived, that was Freddy's —*

THE KITCHEN. HELENE IS ON THE PHONE.

HELENE   : Not till later? But you know, I made this
                reservation. Well, I guess it's okay. Alright, it's
                important? Well, I'll call Bernard. I'm sure it's
                fine . . . I think Wolfgang made a little cake. I
                mean he — he thinks — yeah. It's going to be
                special. So you will — yeah, if you can come
                by 9:30, that would be great. Okay. Okay, 9:30
                it is. Okay, darling. I'm sorry, but that — it'll
                be great, it'll be perfect. Okay. I love you, too.
                (She hangs up)

THE GARDEN TABLE.

SOPHIE   : You know what happens to me after a year
                and a half?

KATE   : What?

SOPHIE   : I just can't have sex with somebody after a year and a half. I get bored. I mean, do you have great sex with your husband after 12 years?

KATE   : (Laughs) I have the *best* sex after 12 years. I just get better.

SOPHIE   : (Laughs) You slut! (They both laugh)

HELENE COMES OUT OF THE HOUSE
AND JOINS THEM, NERVOUS AND EXCITED.

HELENE   : Hi.

KATE   : Hi.

HELENE   : Nothing's ready yet. But can I get you something?

THE LIVING ROOM. ANOTHER OF THE YOUNG WOMEN,
JENNIFER, IS BEING INTERVIEWED. SHE LOOKS DIRECTLY AT US.

JENNIFER   : *I've never been able to hold a job, a boyfriend, nothing . . . my father's attention . . . And food is there, it's accessible, it's easy . . . With men, I have trouble eating, I don't know what it is, so I — you know, I could get very skinny if I'm in a long relationship . . . I have trouble eating in front of people I like . . . So I might hold something in my mouth for a long time, before I chew it. Or I might not eat, if I'm having dinner with somebody and they're looking at me and I have the food in my mouth, so, you know, mm hmm, and then I might try and swallow it . . .*
. . . I think it's erotic. It's safe sex. I mean it's the safest sex you can have, eating. (She laughs)

OUTSIDE AT THE GARDEN TABLE. HELENE IS STANDING,
TALKING TO SOPHIE AND KATE.

HELENE   : I'm so worried about this cake . . . They
                haven't come . . . I should have made a cake.
                I mean, I'm a *great* cakemaker, I went to school
                for three years to learn to make chocolate
                tortes. The last time I made a chocolate torte,
                Frank said, 'cause the sun melted a little tiny bit
                of it, he said, "That looks awful." Do you know
                what he did? He put it in the trash, he went to
                the bakery and he got another one that *looked*
                good . . . I vowed I would *never* make another
                chocolate torte . . . . I *so* wanted to give this
                party, to give myself a good send-off, to give
                you a good send-off and *Sadie* a good send-off in
                our next decade of life . . . Oh, and now I don't
                know — I just feel like I'm crazy and I don't
                know what's going to happen to me. I mean,
                I don't know what's going to happen in the
                next five years. What's going on, you know?
                I feel like I'm just this ship, kind of lost . . .
                Oh well . . . And my *hair* . . . (She laughs)
                You know, I wish I could get new hair for my
                birthday . . . (Kate laughs)

THE LIVING ROOM. A THIRD YOUNG WOMAN
IS BEING INTERVIEWED. HER NAME IS WALLI.

WALLI   : *I went from cocaine to wheat grass . . .*
                Fat is bad, thin is good . . . Sometimes I feel fat,
                I don't know. I try to think that being rounder
                is being feminine. And being a stick figure is
                for drawings and not for people . . .

OUTSIDE, AT THE GARDEN TABLE.

HELENE   : I never felt that I would ever hit 40. I just
                never thought I would *get* here, you know?
                It just seemed, when my mom was 40, it just
                seemed like she was so *old*, you know,
                it seemed like the end of the world . . .
                Oh God, do you think we'll live through this? . . .
                (She laughs, starts to leave) I'm going to check
                everybody, okay?

SOPHIE   : Calm down.

KATE   : Is there anything we can do to help?

HELENE   : No, just have fun. (She runs off)

SOPHIE   : She's completely hysterical.

KATE   : Well, poor baby, why not. I mean she's
                doing this incredible party.

SOPHIE   : Yeah, well, she's got some *real* problems.

THE DEN. MARTINE IS SITTING ON THE FLOOR WITH LYDIA,
WHO IS READING HER PALM.

LYDIA   : You've got a *very* long life line.

MARTINE   : Don't do that.

LYDIA   : What?

MARTINE   : I want to think that my future is open.

LYDIA   : It is. Your palm changes with everything you do.

MARTINE   : Really?

LYDIA   : Yep. You make your own future.

MARTINE   : Hm. That's good.

LYDIA   : Yes, it *is* good.

MARTINE   : How long have your father and your stepmother
               been married?

LYDIA   : Oh, ten years. They got married when I was
               nine years old.

MARTINE   : Your stepmother is wonderful, no?

LYDIA   : Yes.

MARTINE   : You like her, yes?

LYDIA   : Yes, I do, of course. I love her.

MARTINE   : She's wonderful.

LYDIA   : Yeah.

MARTINE   : I was never close to my father . . . That's a
               shame . . .

LYDIA   : What kind of man was he?

MARTINE   : Well, very, kind of, you know, *cold* man.
               Was nice, I mean, was nothing wrong about
               him, but just he was very removed, you know.
               I don't know, he was just very cold and was
               working a lot and I didn't see him very much.

LYDIA   : When I was growing up, I was Daddy's Little Girl, you know?

MARTINE   : Must be very nice to be close to your father.

LYDIA   : Yeah. I just had to learn to watch out for myself, because I was always there for him and he took advantage of that . . . Do you like my dad?

MARTINE   : Yes. I think he's really nice.

LYDIA   : Yeah. You two seem to really get along, you know.

MARTINE   : Well, my father has talked about him so much, you know . . . he really likes him so much.

THE FRONT DOOR. HELENE RUNS TO OPEN IT.
IT IS HER SISTER, NANCY, LADEN WITH GIFTS.

NANCY   : Happy birthday, sis!

HELENE   : Oh, I can't believe it.

NANCY   : Well, I did a little shopping, you know me.

THE TWO SISTERS WALK TO THE STAIRCASE
AND SIT DOWN.

NANCY   : Oh, darling, it's so nice to see you.

HELENE   : Let me sit down and look at you . . . all these presents . . .

NANCY   : I know, I hope you like them. I think you will.

HELENE   : You look so wonderful.

NANCY   : Do you really think so?

HELENE   : Yes, but you have such pretty hair. You
               shouldn't put it behind your head. It should
               be around your face.

NANCY   : (Laughs) *Thank* you! That's so *kind* of you!
               Always a kind *word* !

HELENE   : And you look like you've gotten a little
               plump.

NANCY   : Oh my God. (She hides her face in her hands)

HELENE   : Have you?

NANCY   : How can you *say* that to me? You know how
               I *am* about these things, but *thank* you. *Thank*
               you! You are *right*! Do you know how many
               times a day I ask people, "Do you think I'm
               fat?" And they say, "No!". . . You're right . . .

THE DEN. HELENE'S MOTHER IS SITTING IN A LARGE CHAIR.
LYDIA, HELENE'S STEPDAUGHTER, JOINS HER.

LYDIA   : Grammy!

MRS. WILLIAMS : Hi, sweet thing.

LYDIA   : Hi. (They kiss)

MRS. WILLIAMS : Glad to see you.

LYDIA : I missed you.

MRS. WILLIAMS : I missed *you.*

THE STAIRCASE. HELENE AND HER SISTER NANCY.

HELENE : Darling, mother is here. I *do* want you not to monopolize her today. *Please.* Just for me, just for me. I know that you want to talk to her, but it's *my* birthday.

NANCY : Oh, I know.

HELENE : Please.

NANCY : I won't, I really won't. I won't.

HELENE : It's my day.

NANCY: : I know. Besides, it won't matter. She — she pays more attention to you anyway.

HELENE : She does not.

NANCY : Always has.

HELENE : She has *never.* (Nancy laughs)

THE DEN. LYDIA IS SITTING ON THE EDGE OF HER STEP-GRANDMOTHER'S CHAIR.

MRS. WILLIAMS : How are you doing with, um . . . your diet?

LYDIA : Yeah, my diet.

MRS. WILLIAMS : Well, I mean your — your way of eating, whatever you call it.

LYDIA   : Well, I still can't eat with Chips and dad.
                   I still can't, you know, sit down at the table with
                   them.

MRS. WILLIAMS : Why can't you eat with them?

LYDIA   : They want everything to be *perfect*. And
                   every time I take a bite of their food, it's like
                   eating what they *believe*, do you know what I'm
                   saying? It's like sitting down to a table and —
                   and eating their *ideals*. And when I get up from
                   the table, I just can't deal with it, you know? It
                   makes me feel like I'm a cornered animal in a
                   cage, you know, just going round and round.

MRS. WILLIAMS : Are these feeling *always* present?

LYDIA   : Not when I'm dancing . . . Not when I'm
                   dancing . . . But it's only when I'm dancing, you
                   know, *not* before and *not* after, but when I'm
                   dancing. It's what we call finding our *center*.
                   And when you just hit that arabesque and you
                   have it. Or a turn, you know, when you turn
                   and you just *have* that center and you . . .
                   (She sighs and shakes her head, unable to finish
                   her sentence)

THE LIVING ROOM. SOPHIE AND HELENE ARE EACH
HOLDING A LARGE, SOFT, PADDED CLUB.

HELENE   : What kind of a birthday present is this?

SOPHIE   : They're *batakas*.

HELENE   : *Batakas*? What's that?

| SOPHIE | : They're tools. They help you get out your anger, you know? Your suppressed anger, your rage? (Helene laughs) Come here. Come on. Come on, hit me. *Hit* me! |

HELENE : Wait, I don't —

SOPHIE : Hit me, *hit* me. Like this. See? (She hits her club against Helene's)

HELENE : Sophie!

SOPHIE : (Hitting her club harder against Helene's) I hate you . . . I — *hate* — you. Say it back!

HELENE : Okay. "I hate you."

SOPHIE : More. Commit. I *hate* you!

HELENE : I hate you . . . I hate you . . .

SOPHIE : More. *More.*

HELENE & SOPHIE : (Together) I hate you . . . I hate you . . . I hate you . . .

SOPHIE : (Really getting into it) You ass-hole . . . You ass . . . hole! I - hate - you . . . (They exhaust themselves, hitting and shouting. After a while, they wear themselves out.) It works . . . it works, doesn't it?

HELENE : I don't know.

SOPHIE : Let's hope it works. (She puts her arm around Helene as they try to catch their breath)

THE HALLWAY. SADIE AND HER DAUGHTER JENNIFER.

SADIE   : I beg of you, don't do this to me. Please,
                 baby, I love you. Don't do this to me.

JENNIFER   : Listen. Listen!

SADIE   : I want you to have a good life.

JENNIFER   : I love you. (They hug and kiss; Jennifer
                 pulls back)

JENNIFER   : I want to tell you something. I want to be an
                 actress. I really want to be an actress.

SADIE   : Oh God, don't want to be an actress, *please*.

JENNIFER   : With all my heart, I want to be an actress.
                 Please help me.

HELENE OPENS THE FRONT DOOR.
TWO FRIENDS ENTER, BEA AND CORY.

BEA : (Laughing) *"Pig!"*

HELENE : (Laughing) I'll get you for that.

BEA : (Shows Helene birthday card) *"To Pig, Love Always, Whaletail!"* (They roar with laughter; the other woman feels left out) You know, we were debutantes together. I'm going to tell the whole party. You know what she did when we went off to school? She rode a bus all the way to school because she didn't want anybody to know she was rich enough to take an airplane. She didn't think anybody else could afford to fly in an airplane.

CORY : (Mock serious) *Really* . . .

OUTSIDE. SOME WOMEN ARE IN THE POOL,
SOME ARE SUNBATHING IN CHAIRS AROUND IT.
HELENE'S MOTHER EXITS THE HOUSE AND WALKS TO
WHERE HER OTHER DAUGHTER, NANCY, IS SITTING,
FULLY COVERED, UNDER AN UMBRELLA.

MRS. WILLIAMS : (Walking) Hi.

WOMEN IN POOL: Hi. Hi . . .

MRS. WILLIAMS : The water cold?

ONE WOMAN : It's a little chilly.

MRS. WILLIAMS : (Laughs) I'll bet . . . (She walks to Nancy and sits down next to her) Hi, Nancy.

NANCY : Hi, mommy. You look so beautiful.

MRS. WILLIAMS : Thank you. So do you. I like your dress.

NANCY   : You do?

MRS. WILLIAMS : Got my favorite color on.

NANCY   : You don't think I look a little fat in it?

MRS. WILLIAMS : Of course you don't look — oh, you girls . . .

THE FRONT DOOR. HELENE IS GREETING
TWO FRIENDS OF SADIE'S, ELOISE AND CATHY.

ELOISE   : Happy birthday. We love you.

HELENE   : Oh, thank you.

ELOISE   : Is Sadie here?

HELENE   : Yes, yes she is. She is.

ELOISE   : Where do we go?

HELENE   : She's in the living room. Here, I'll show
                 you . . . (They follow her)

UNDER THE UMBRELLA, BY THE POOL.
NANCY AND HER MOTHER.

MRS. WILLIAMS : I don't know what to do with you girls about
                 this *food* business and about *fat* and —

NANCY   : I know, I know, I know.

MRS. WILLIAMS : You have a *lovely* figure.

NANCY   : I know, but not like *them*. (She points to a
                 few women in bathing suits)

MRS. WILLIAMS : (Looks at the other women) No, you're about the same size as a matter of fact.

NANCY   : Yeah . . .

KATE SWIMS UP TO THE EDGE OF THE POOL.
SHE IS TINY IN A BIKINI, SMILING BROADLY.

KATE   : Hi.

NANCY   : Hi.

KATE SWIMS OFF. NANCY'S MOTHER LOOKS AFTER HER.

MRS. WILLIAMS : Well now *that's* — that's *exceptional* . . .

NANCY   : Yeah. (They both laugh)

MRS. WILLIAMS : But she probably starves herself. Or she does that awful thing some of you do . . . You don't do that do you? . . . I mean you eat a lot to make yourself throw up so you don't gain weight? You don't do that.

NANCY   : Well, I —

MRS. WILLIAMS : You *don't* do *that*, do you?

NANCY   : Well, not *chronically*, no, but, you know, I have.

MRS. WILLIAMS : What do you mean, not chronically? You mean you *have*?

NANCY   : Yes!

MRS. WILLIAMS : Oh, Nancy, that's kind of sick.

NANCY   : I know, it *is*. I don't want to do it and I don't
                 do it very often, mommy. It's just that, you
                 know I just —I — I'm just too big, and you
                 know, Jim likes me so thin, and . . .

MRS. WILLIAMS : Oh, Nancy, you're not big. There must be
                 something wrong with you and Jim. Are you
                 having problems?

NANCY   : With Mr. Commodities? (She laughs) Well,
                 it's getting a little dull, ma. (They laugh)

MRS. WILLIAMS : Well, at least he's successful at it. And he
                 gives you a good living. You know, the way
                 you love to shop.

NANCY   : I know, but I'm just shopping in thrift stores
                 for funky clothes, and he thinks I should be
                 shopping at Chanel and I —

MRS. WILLIAMS : Funky clothes? Aren't those new? They're
                 beautiful. (She holds Nancy's ears, looks at
                 her earrings.)

NANCY   : Yeah . . .

MRS. WILLIAMS : Emeralds? Diamonds? I don't call *those* funky.

NANCY   : (Smiles) I know.

THE FRONT DOOR. HELENE ANSWERS IT. JACKIE ENTERS.

HELENE   : Hi.

JACKIE   : Hel*een*?

HELENE   : Hel*e*ne Bradley.

JACKIE   : Hi. I'm Sadie's friend, you called me about her birthday? I'm Jackie?

HELENE   : Oh, yes. Jackie. Jackie, hi —

JACKIE   : I don't have a present.

HELENE   : She's in the living room.

JACKIE   : Happy birthday.

UNDER THE UMBRELLA. NANCY AND HER MOTHER.

NANCY   : You always thought that Helene was perfect because she was so thin.

MRS. WILLIAMS : So it's this sibling rivalry.

NANCY   : Well, mommy, it's *true*.

MRS. WILLIAMS : Oh, it's just because it's her birthday today and she's the focus of attention.

NANCY   : No that isn't it. I've never been like that. It's just that, you know, she's *always* been thin and she's *always* been perfect and — Oh God, I'm sorry to do this, I'm not going to do it.

MRS. WILLIAMS : Oh, Nancy . . .

NANCY   : I really miss you and I love seeing you, and . . .

MRS. WILLIAMS : . . . It doesn't seem like that . . .

NANCY   : . . . I would *love* to be as thin as Helene.

MRS. WILLIAMS : Why is that so all-*important*?

THE FRONT DOOR. HELENE IS WITH MARIA AND MILLIE.
THEY HAVE BROUGHT A GIFT, A METALLIC BALL THAT
OPENS IN HALVES, WITH PADDING INSIDE.

MILLIE   : Okay now, you do *this*, okay? (She demonstrates
                      the "Scream Ball" by screaming into it)

MARIA   : Yes, you'll never get cancer this way.

(MILLIE SCREAMS INTO SCREAM BALL.)

MARIA   : Ease up . . . Ease up . . .

MILLIE   : (Handing Scream Ball to Helene) Try it . . .
                      try it . . .

(HELENE SCREAMS A POWERFUL SCREAM INTO THE
METAL BALL.)

MARIA   : Good. Get it out! Get it out!

(HELENE SCREAMS AGAIN.)

MARIA   : Fabulous. Fabulous.

MILLIE   : Your cheeks are all pink. Don't you feel better?

(HELENE SCREAMS INTO THE BALL AGAIN.)

MARIA   : She's going to be very good at this.
                      Very good at this.

MILLIE   : Forty isn't that hard.

(HELENE TURNS AND HEADS BACK TO THE PARTY,
STILL SCREAMING INTO THE BALL.)

MARIA   : Go with it honey, go, go, *go* !

POOLSIDE. SITTING TOGETHER ARE
SADIE, ELOISE AND ELOISE'S FRIEND, CATHY.

ELOISE   : This is my agent, Sadie. Sadie, MCM.

CATHY   : Hi.

SADIE   : Nice meeting you.

ELOISE   : Okay, here's your gift.

SADIE   : A gift for me? Another *chachka*?

ELOISE   : I don't want you to open it, I just want you to
                  read the card.

SADIE   : Let me see what you have to say. Alright,
                  what's going on?

ANOTHER PART OF POOLSIDE.
HELENE'S MOTHER IS NOW SITTING NEXT TO SOPHIE,
WHO IS EATING OUT OF A STYROFOAM CONTAINER.
CONNIE IS SERVING WINE.

MRS. WILLIAMS : Why are eating out of that tacky container?

CONNIE   : Would you like some wine?

SOPHIE   : No, thank you.

MRS. WILLIAMS : No, no thanks . . .
                  (To Sophie) My daughter has some very
                  attractive china. Is she serving food in this?

SOPHIE   : No, no, this is special *macrobiotic* food that
                  I had sent in. So that I could have something to
                  eat here, because I don't eat this horrible food
                  that she serves.

MRS. WILLIAMS : What do you *mean*, horrible food?

SOPHIE   : It's greasy and it's got sugar in it and butter.
              You know what that kind of food does?
              It makes you old and ugly-looking very early
              on, quick. Now wait a minute. *You're*
              different. I mean *you* happen to be —

MRS. WILLIAMS : (She laughs) I'm not that different.

SOPHIE   : — You are blessed with the most perfect
              constitution I've ever seen.

ANOTHER PART OF POOLSIDE.

SADIE   : (Reading Eloise's card) "You can buy a
              house and I'll take a trip to a far off land, where
              men love women," *alright* ". . . who have meat
              on their bones and room in their hearts, for
              someone besides themselves. I can't do this
              alone, Sadie my sweet. Stay by my side. I love
              you. Eloise!" *Alright.* (She kisses Eloise)
              You're wonderful, Angel. What a sweet thing.
              Can I? I won't open it now.

ELOISE   : No, I want you to save it, it's real personal.
              I want to take you somewhere.

SADIE   : Where?

ELOISE   : I don't know. Where do you want to go?

SADIE   : Well, I want to go some place where the men
              are, just like you wrote about, who love women
              with meat on their bones.

ELOISE   : Tell me where. Where do you want to go?

SADIE   : Ummm . . . La Costa!

UNDER THE UMBRELLA, POOLSIDE.
HELENE'S MOTHER AND SOPHIE, DEEP IN TALK.

SOPHIE : . . . I'm very worried about her. I mean, she's obviously having problems with that horrible, horrible husband of hers who thinks he's a feminist and really can't bear women.

MRS. WILLIAMS : Well, I've never been that crazy about Frank, but is he that —

SOPHIE : He's *terrible*. I mean, he's beautiful, he's gorgeous and he's just charming, but he needs to control . . . She listens to him, she thinks that he has these answers, because *why*? Because he's a *therapist*? As if therapists have *answers*?

KATE SWIMS UP TO JOIN THEM.

KATE : Hi. Can I join you?

SOPHIE : Darling, do you mind? I just want to talk to her for a minute.

KATE : Oh, I'm sorry Sophie.

KATE SWIMS AWAY.

SOPHIE : Happy birthday!

MRS. WILLIAMS : Oh, it's *her* birthday, too?

SOPHIE : She's still cute, isn't she?

MRS. WILLIAMS : She's adorable.

SOPHIE : She's got a few years more, looking like that.

MRS. WILLIAMS : Sophie, everything you say, there's such a negative connotation.

SOPHIE   : Oh, you're right . . . I shouldn't be this negative. I really don't want to be, and from now on I'm not going to be, you're right. But I — I'm really concerned about Helene and I think *that's* why I'm this way and it's *eating* at me.

ANOTHER PART OF POOLSIDE.

SADIE   : (Looking at card) How sweet . . . I love it . . .

ELOISE   : Happy birthday.

SADIE   : Thank you . . . I *hate* this birthday.

JENNIFER, SADIE'S DAUGHTER, WALKS UP TO THEM.

JENNIFER   : Hi.

SADIE   : (Kisses her) My baby. I love you.

THE FRONT DOOR. HELENE RUNS TO ANSWER IT.
MOLLY, A PAINTER, AND HER TWO MODELS ENTER.

MOLLY   : Helene, happy birthday . . . Darling, these are my two new models . . . This is Lee and this is Janice and (indicating painting), *this* is one of the old girls, you'll recognize as soon as you see her.

HELENE   : Oh, I can't wait . . . Are you going to open it right here?

BACK AT POOLSIDE.

JENNIFER : I've got to talk to you, mother.

SADIE : Honey, please, it's bad enough I'm turning 50. No confrontations today.

JENNIFER : Ma, I've got to talk to you.

SADIE : Please, *not now*! Honey, you'll get over this and we'll talk later. Alright?

JENNIFER : Okay, fine. (She walks off in a huff, muttering) . . . I can't believe it . . .

SADIE : Oh God, I love her so much, but they drive you crazy.

CATHY : How old is she?

SADIE : *Too* old. You know, she was an old woman from the minute she was born. She came out of the *womb* an old woman. She's always had the beat on me.

THE HALLWAY. HELENE AND HER SISTER, NANCY.

NANCY : No, no, you didn't upset me. It's just that I'm a little upset. I've been just having some funny thoughts lately. I've been kind of restless, you know, about Jim and everything.

BACK AT POOLSIDE.

SADIE : I hate turning 50. I'm so depressed.

CATHY : You don't *look* 50. I mean you look —

SADIE   : It doesn't make it any better.

ELOISE   : I mean, how old do I look?

SADIE   : Let's not talk about it. I have a new deal
                 cooking for you.

ELOISE   : What?

SADIE   : You've got to look young.

ELOISE   : A new deal?

SADIE   : I'm not going to tell you about it. It's *so* exciting.

THE HALLWAY.
NANCY AND HELENE ARE STANDING BY THE MIRROR.

NANCY   : . . . It's just that life is getting so *dull* with
                 him. And I — I met this man at a party.

HELENE   : You *didn't?*

NANCY   : Yes. And he's an actor. And he's really *poor.*
                 And I've been having these sort of fantasies
                 lately that, I don't know, maybe we could
                 starve together. (She laughs)

POOLSIDE. KATE IS IN THE WATER.
MRS. WILLIAMS IS SITTING ALONE.

MRS. WILLIAMS : Katie, you look adorable.

KATE   : Oh, thanks.

MRS. WILLIAMS : Good color, too. But don't get *too*
                 much sun.

KATE   : I won't.

MARTINE WALKS TOWARD THEM.

MARTINE   : How's the water, Kate?

KATE   : Oh, it's great.

MARTINE   : Good . . . (She sits down. Kate swims off.)
                       Hello, Mrs. Williams, my name is Martine. Nice
                       to meet you. (They shake hands)

MRS. WILLIAMS : It's nice to meet *you.* Oh, you're staying here
                       with them?

MARTINE   : Yes, Helene told you I was staying here, you
                       know, because I'm making a documentary for
                       French television.

MRS. WILLIAMS : Oh, are you?

MARTINE   : Yes . . . You know, when Helene and Frank
                       went to France after their wedding? —

MRS. WILLIAMS : — Yes?

MARTINE   : They stayed at my parents. Mr. and Mrs.
                       Monnier?

MRS. WILLIAMS : Oh, that's right. Of course.

MARTINE   : So, they asked me to stay at their place.

MRS. WILLIAMS : You are a gorgeous young French lady, I
                       must say.

MARTINE   : (Embarrassed) Thank you.

MRS. WILLIAMS : It's true.

MARTINE   : I wish I could feel that. I don't feel gorgeous.

MRS. WILLIAMS : *You* don't feel gorgeous?

MARTINE   : (Blushing) Not at all.

MRS. WILLIAMS : Look at you. I mean you're just *perfection,* so
                I don't know *why.* I wish you could *feel* what I *see.*

MARTINE   : Well, especially, you know, this whole
               thing makes me so nervous. You know, this
               all-woman party? It's so strange . . . I always
               felt very uncomfortable with women . . .

MRS. WILLIAMS : Any threat from other women? Is that it?

MARTINE   : I don't know if it's threats, just that, you
               know, they look at me and I just feel big
               and I don't feel secure, I feel, I don't know.
               I have this *thing,* because I don't like the way
               I look, I always feel very uncomfortable . . .
               When I'm with men, sometimes, I can feel
               beautiful. But among women, I always felt like,
               you know, because I'm *big* . . .

MRS. WILLIAMS : Don't tell me even in *Fran*ce you have this
                thing about *food? Eating* food? . . .
                Of course, you have such wonderful food in
                France.

THE FRONT DOOR. HELENE IS BEING GREETED BY THREE
FRIENDS. ONE OF THEM HANDS HER A PRESENT.

CHRIS   : How are you? Happy birthday. I brought
               you something, if you need centering, open
               that, okay?

POOLSIDE.

MARTINE : I hate my cheeks. You know, I always wanted to have these Marlene Dietrich cheeks—

MRS. WILLIAMS : (Feels Martine's face) That's what we call good bones . . .

MARTINE : You know, Marlene Dietrich . . . these cheeks like that? (She sucks them in)

MRS. WILLIAMS : (Laughs) I wanted so much to be the high-fashion model with those sunken-cheeks you're talking about. But the editors at *Vogue* hated me, I looked so healthy and not sunken-cheeked. So instead of doing high-fashion things, I ended up being the *personality* model: "Use Ipana Toothpaste!" "Smoke Chesterfields!" . . . I got so tired of smiling . . .

THE FRONT DOOR. MORE GREETINGS FOR HELENE.

RUTH   : Happy birthday. You look beautiful.

HELENE   : Thank you, sweetheart.

ANITA   : Happy birthday.

HELENE   : Thank you. (She opens presents)

POOLSIDE. KATE JOINS MRS. WILLIAMS AND MARTINE.

KATE   : Hi.

MARTINE   : Hi . . . *This* is the kind of woman I would like
                  to be, you know.

KATE   : Oh, please.

MARTINE   : This kind of skinny, thin, tiny,
                  wonderful-looking . . .

KATE   : Says *she* with those legs . . . up to my
                  shoulders.

MARTINE   : I don't like it.

MRS. WILLIAMS : You see, just what she said, she'd like to have
                  your legs up to *her* shoulders.

KATE   : When I was dancing I dreamed about legs
                  like those. That was my greatest fantasy.

MRS. WILLIAMS : Great dancer's legs . . . I don't know what
                  any of you expect. You're just perfection.

ANOTHER PART OF POOLSIDE.
ELOISE SHOWS SADIE A BOOK.

ELOISE : I want you to read this.

SADIE : I've read it.

ELOISE : Well, Robert Redford has the rights to it, and I just want to play the part of Lila. It's *wonderful*.

SADIE : Well, I'll see if you can.

ELOISE : Yes, I want you to get in touch with him.

SADIE : I'll have the literary department check it out.

ELOISE : Sadie, I don't want you to have the literary department get a hold of it. I want *you* to do it.

SADIE : Why are you making a . . . this is my birthday party. Why do we have to discuss Robert Redford and the rights to this movie?

ANOTHER PART OF POOLSIDE. SOPHIE IS STILL EATING MACROBIOTIC. JENNIFER, NEXT TO HER, IS PICKING AT IT.

SOPHIE : Four years ago I let go of my mother, who's exactly like yours. Evil, toxic, destructive . . .

JENNIFER : My mother's not toxic. She just doesn't represent me. I want her to represent me. You know, she's an agent.

SOPHIE : You don't need your mother to make it as an actress. I mean, your mother doesn't even want you to *be* successful.

JENNIFER   : My mother does *too* want me to be successful.

SOPHIE   : Your mother *hates* you.

JENNIFER   : You don't even *know* my mother.

SOPHIE   : Jennifer, I have the same mother.

JENNIFER   : No you don't.

SOPHIE   : Oh, yes I do. I have the exact same mother as your mother. They're both *vulgarians.*

ANOTHER PART OF POOLSIDE.
MARTINE IS FILMING CATHY AS ELOISE AND MARIA WATCH.

CATHY   : Do I get paid for this?

ELOISE   : Do you get *paid* for this? (She laughs)

THE DINING ROOM. NEXT TO THE DINING TABLE,
WHERE FOOD AND PLATES ARE BEING LAID OUT,
SIT MILLIE AND DR. BENSON, A PLASTIC SURGEON.

MILLIE   : Dr. Benson, isn't there something you can do to help me?

DR. BENSON : What's been done? What was your problem?

MILLIE   : I've had them done *every* way.

DR. BENSON : Well, *what* did you have done? What was the procedure?

MILLIE   : *Every*thing.

DR. BENSON : Bigger, smaller?

MILLIE : Bigger.

DR. BENSON : Mmhmm.

MILLIE : I had them done the first time, and then, within three months, they were like this. (She picks up an apple) *Baseballs.* I was sleeping on *baseballs.*

DR. BENSON : Did you massage afterwards? You didn't massage?

MILLIE : No.

DR. BENSON : Did your doctor tell you to?

MILLIE : No. I just had them redone. Then I had them redone *another* way. Then I had them redone *another* way. This has been going on for *12 years.*

DR. BENSON : The same surgeon?

MILLIE : No. I went to different ones.

DR. BENSON : Different ones?

MILLIE : Different styles. I never did go to a *woman* surgeon, though. Maybe *that's* what I should do, you know?

DR. BENSON : Well. You just need to go to a *good* surgeon. I'd have to *see* your breasts. I'd have to see exactly what the problem is. You have to come in.

MILLIE   : Okay . . . Alright . . . Do you think I should have a face lift? Maybe *that* would fix it. (She pulls back the sides of her face)

DR. BENSON   : (Laughs) Let's do one thing at a time. We'll get that part handled first.

MOLLY HAS WALKED IN BETWEEN THEM.

MOLLY   : Having your face done?

MILLIE   : Maybe. Do you think I need it?

MOLLY   : *No* !

MILLIE   : No? Just a little here. Don't you think?

MOLLY   : No, no, no. (To Dr. Benson) Do *you* think she needs anything?

DR. BENSON   : Well, she has other things she has to deal with *first*, I think.

MOLLY   : What?

DR. BENSON   : You could use your eyes, your lower eyes.

MILLIE   : Could I? (She pulls at her eyes)

POOLSIDE. MARTINE IS FILMING MARIA NOW.

MARIA   : (Into the camera, making a message for Helene) *Forty is fabulous! Happy birthday!*

MARTINE   : Thank you.

MARIA : I should be taking pictures of *you*. You're actually quite wonderful with that camera in your hand. (She pulls out her camera) Great. Great, sweetheart. Keep it moving . . . Keep it moving . . . (She snaps photos; they all pose) Great. You could never keep out of the spotlight. Okay, Sadie, there you go. Great, great, great . . .

THE DEN.
JENNIFER AND LYDIA ARE SITTING BY THE FIREPLACE.

JENNIFER : My mother's having this affair with this man, and he really likes *me*. He's young, he's like 35 or younger. And he really likes me. I mean he sneaks me food and stuff like that.

LYDIA : Well, that's not the ultimate romantic gesture. (She laughs)

JENNIFER : Yeah, but he likes me. He feeds me. You know when men feed you they like you . . . She told him she was *40*.

LYDIA : So?

JENNIFER : So, I think she's going through menopause. She's really afraid of being 50. And he likes me and she thinks he likes her and I *know* when he looks at me, he just, you know . . . (She smiles)

LYDIA : Well, have there been any advances or what? *Besides* food.

JENNIFER : Well, he just devours me with his eyes. You know, he just looks over the table at me.

LYDIA   : Well, yeah, but looking is different. I mean
               it's like, you can look at hors d'oeuvres and not
               taste them, you know.

POOLSIDE.

SADIE   : I've got to accept it, I'm 50, I'm getting old
               and the parade's going by.

MARIA   : Stop it. You don't smoke, you don't eat,
               you've got a great body. Look at those *ankles*,
               sweetheart.

SADIE   : (Lifts up an ankle) Do you like my ankles?

MARIA   : They're *holding* . . . I mean I think you're in a
               holding pattern, myself, you know?

SADIE   : We'll see what happens next. I have no idea
               what's going to happen next. I'll probably die
               before I'm 51.

MARIA   : What happened to that little fellow you were into?

SADIE : I'm not into little fellows any more. Just big ones! (They both laugh)

THE DEN, BY THE FIREPLACE.

LYDIA : Is he *sleeping* with her? That's the question.

JENNIFER : Well, I don't listen at their door.

LYDIA : Well I mean, does he stay over?

JENNIFER : Yeah, he stays over.

LYDIA : Well —

JENNIFER : But the lights go off and there's no *music*, you know, from her room. And she doesn't look very *happy* in the morning, you know. She's all growly and calling her clients and everything. I think he's with her because he's an actor and, you know, he thinks that he's going to get work from her . . . I don't know why I did it, but I told him. I told him that she was *50*. I mean he asked me, I just *had* to tell him. You know, he said, what's this party about tonight? And I said well, it's my mother's 50th birthday. And he just looked at me like, *what*?

LYDIA : Don't you think that's sabotaging her a little bit? I mean —

JENNIFER : Well, it's the *fact* . . . She sabotaged *my* life.

LYDIA : Yeah, but —

JENNIFER : I didn't mean to . . . Look, I just said the truth . . . He's young enough to be *my* boyfriend . . .

EXTERIOR. A GARDEN TABLE. JACKIE AND ELOISE.

JACKIE   : I've got great news and I'm totally depressed.

ELOISE   : Why?

JACKIE   : Don't tell Sadie. Sam Cohn wants to handle me.

ELOISE   : Sam Cohn wants to handle *you*?

JACKIE   : Yeah. You say that so surprised.

ELOISE   : Are you serious? He wants to handle you?

JACKIE   : *Yes*!

ELOISE   : What are you going to do?

JACKIE   : What do you mean what am I going to do? I've got to make a move.

ELOISE   : Make a move. That's what you do, you make a move. Sam Cohn is the biggest agent in the world.

JACKIE   : I know, it's real easy, you put one foot in front of the other and then you're finally out the door . . .

ELOISE   : Right.

JACKIE   : How do I tell Sadie?

ELOISE   : You write her a letter, you give her a present, and you go with Sam Cohn. And then you take me with you!

ANOTHER PART OF THE GARDEN. KATE AND MARTINE
AT A TABLE. BEHIND THEM IS THE POOL,
WITH SOME OF THE WOMEN IN AND AROUND IT.

KATE : I always dreamed that one day I would grow a foot and have long beautiful legs.

MARTINE : Yeah, I always dreamt to be a tiny, delicate, young girl. You know, the one people want to take care of. Because *nobody* ever wanted to take care of me, you know? I always was so big and so strong and I was the one who carried the suitcases. Nobody would ever help me, because I was so strong. And I wanted to be protected and to be tiny and delicate and little.

KATE : I was so into being strong that even if they wanted to carry my suitcases, I wouldn't *let* them.

MARTINE : You know, doctors always have told me, well, you — how do you say that — you are designed to be a mother? I mean you are made, your body is just *made* to be a mother.

KATE : 'Cause you're so female.

MARTINE : Sure, yeah, I've got these big hips and it's just perfect to have babies . . . I don't *like* big hips.

THE FRONT DOOR. CECE AND LESLIE GREET HELENE.
CECE HAS MANY PRESENTS AND HANDS THEM ONE BY
ONE TO HELENE.

CECE : This is for *you* . . . This is for *Sadie* . . . This is for *Sophie*, so she doesn't feel left out . . . This is for the girl I don't *know* . . . This is my friend, *Leslie*.

HELENE   : Hi, Leslie, how are you?

LESLIE   : Happy birthday.

THE GARDEN TABLE.

KATE   : My mother told me over and over when I was
              growing up, she said, "Darling, it's so wonderful
              because *your* generation doesn't *have* to have
              children . . ." It just made me feel like shit . . .
              I understood that *we* were something that she
              felt that she should do. And did *beautifully*.
              But the end result was that we ruined her life in
              some way that she subliminally resented us for,
              or whatever. And I just know that — I know
              that if I have kids, I want to *want* them, so
              much . . .

MARTINE   : Have you ever been pregnant?

KATE   : . . . Yeah, I got pregnant when I was 18,
              with my husband, who was then my boyfriend.
              And I had an abortion. Because I knew I wasn't
              ready and so, it was okay . . . But I remember it
              being the strangest experience, because he was
              there holding my hand, and the doctor that gave
              me the abortion was a woman, and her name
              was *Chastity*. And she was about seven months
              pregnant. And I remember she was wearing
              this little Peter Pan collar. When she gave me
              the abortion, she said, "This is just *potential*.
              This is not life. This is just potential." And I know
              that it was right, God, I knew I wasn't ready,
              but it was so strange . . . the "potential" . . .
              . . . What about you?

MARTINE : When I had *my* abortion it was terrible. I just
spent two weeks waking up in the morning and
saying to myself, "I will keep it, I want it." And
then, you know, I was at my parents, and my
mother knew about it, and one day I asked her,
— and they wanted me to have an abortion —
and I asked her, but mummy, once it's *there*,
once the baby is *born*, you cannot regret to
have it? And she said, "Well I'm not sure,
maybe you can." And it destroyed me, my
mother saying that, you know? . . . And then I
had this fear of getting pregnant all the time.
Every time I approached a man, I was scared
of getting pregnant. It was like something
completely crazy at one point, you know? That
I was feeling I was gaining weight, and it was
because I was pregnant. I began to starve
myself. I had the feeling that my stomach was
getting big, you know? So I began to starve
myself and I got very skinny . . . But *then* my
period stopped, so it was like being pregnant
again . . . I always thought I would get married
and have children . . . I always was sure of that,
you know . . . And now, I know I will *not* get
married. And I know I will *not* have children.

KATE   : How can you know that?

MARTINE   : I don't know. I'm just — it's the way I feel.
                  I just don't feel I will ever have children . . .

ANOTHER PART OF THE GARDEN. SADIE AND JACKIE.

SADIE   : Do you understand what I want to do for you?
                  I want to do for *you* what they did for Sheena
                  Easton with "Miami Vice." That's what I want to
                  do for you. You'll make so much money . . .

JACKIE   : I *need* to change agents. I need somebody.
                  I've worked so hard, *we've* worked so hard,
                  getting me to a certain spot. I could call the
                  same people that *you* can call now. I need
                  somebody that can take the ball from me.
                  I don't want to make this mistake again.
                  We almost got there once before. And I didn't
                  leave, because I felt this family connection . . .
                  You know you're like family to me . . .

SADIE   : You're killing me. I can't believe this.

JACKIE   : You know, Michael Jackson can fire his father,
                I've *got* to be able to do that! *I've got to*!!

BACK TO THE GARDEN TABLE WITH KATE AND MARTINE.

KATE   : When I was a kid my brothers had my parents
                and I always got the nannies, and so every time
                that I fell in love with one of them, they left.
                And that's why, every single day that I have
                been with this man, and every single year that
                continues to be joyous and wonderful is such a
                miracle . . . I am really afraid, if I am not in-
                credibly careful, I *will* fuck it all up. And *that*
                would probably be — the saddest thing in my
                life. So I do have to be careful. And I do have
                to — to *pretend* that — I believe that — that I
                can grow old with this man. And I can become
                grown-up enough to make children with this
                person. And — and to — to get ugly and —
                and old and — and *die* with this person.

MARTINE   : You know, I really think you shouldn't
                take a chance of ruining your relationship
                by questioning — by questioning *too* much.
                I really think that.

KATE   : Come on, let's go get something to eat. (They
                both laugh)

MARTINE (V.O.): Okay.

LATER. THE LIVING ROOM. ALL THE WOMEN ARE DRESSED
NOW IN THEIR PARTY OUTFITS. THREE YOUNG WOMEN
BRING IN THREE CAKES, ONE FOR EACH OF THE BIRTHDAY
WOMEN. THEY ARE SINGING "HAPPY BIRTHDAY" AND ALL
THE OTHER WOMEN JOIN IN.

THEY PUT THE CAKES DOWN, THE SONG ENDS, THEY
ALL APPLAUD. SOMEBODY SHOUTS "MAKE A WISH" AND
HELENE, KATE AND SADIE EACH BLOWS OUT THE CANDLES
ON HER CAKE. MORE APPLAUSE AND CHEERS. HELENE
CUTS A PIECE OF CAKE AND HANDS IT TO SADIE.

SADIE   : Oh no, no thank you.

HELENE   : Oh, Sadie, I had it made special, it's your
             favorite, it's Swiss chocolate!

SADIE   : I didn't even have cake at my son's wedding.
             No, I couldn't possibly.

HELENE   : It's bad luck.

JENNIFER   : You *must* have it.

SADIE   : No! (To her daughter) And *you* can't have it.
             I don't want *you* to get fat.

HELENE   : (To Kate) Would *you* cut yourself a piece of cake, please, you *must.*

KATE   : I'll cut the cake, but I really don't want a piece right now.

A PLATE WITH A SLICE OF CAKE IS PASSED FROM WOMAN TO WOMAN, MAKING A LARGE CIRCLE. EACH WOMAN PASSES THE CAKE ON, NONE EATS ANY, THEY JUST KEEP TALKING AND PASSING. MARTINE IS FILMING ALL THIS RATHER INTENSELY. SHE IS UNABLE TO TAKE HER EYE — OR HER CAMERA — OFF THE PLATE WITH THE CAKE.

MRS. WILLIAMS : I can't *believe* that no one is eating cake. What's wrong? . . .

MILLIE   : I just can't eat it at all. The last time I had sugar, I ate it for five days straight.

MRS. WILLIAMS : (Eating) Mmmm . . . you don't know what you're missing . . . (To Helene) At least have a piece of your own cake! (Helene refuses it)

KATE OPENS A BOTTLE OF CHAMPAGNE WITH A POP. THERE ARE SCREAMS, CHEERS AND APPLAUSE.

THE STAIRCASE. JENNIFER IS SITTING ALONE ON THE STAIRS,
EATING A PIECE OF CAKE. FROM THE LIVING ROOM WE
HEAR THE VOICES OF THE WOMEN. AFTER A WHILE, SADIE
WALKS OUT, CATCHES JENNIFER EATING ON THE STAIRS.
JENNIFER TRIES TO HIDE THE PLATE, FEELS CAUGHT.

JENNIFER   : Oh!

SADIE   : Oh, my God, honey.

JENNIFER   : What? . . . Oh . . . (She pulls out the hidden
                  plate) Well, I was eating some . . . well, you
                  won't let me eat anything . . . Ma, mommy,
                  don't cry . . .

A COUCH. ELOISE AND HER SISTER, BERRY,
SQUEEZED IN IT TOGETHER, SIDE BY SIDE.

BERRY   : You know I'd much rather be me than you.
                  Because when I'm fat, I *always* think I'm thin.
                  And when you're thin, you *always* think you're fat.

THE DEN. MARTINE IS SETTING UP HER CAMERA
TO INTERVIEW HELENE AND KATE.

MARTINE   : It won't take long. Just relax. Answer a few
                  questions . . . Thank you . . . So, you are eating
                  right now . . .

HELENE   : Oh, alright. (She puts her bread down in her
                  lap)

MARTINE   : (Laughs) Do you have any problem with
                  food?

HELENE   : (She nervously picks the bread up again, talks
                  into the camera) *No, uh, not really* . . .

MARTINE   : Not really?

HELENE   : (Into camera) *No . . .* (Kate smiles)
*But you know something? I like the feel of food.
I like to feel it. I don't like to eat with forks or
knives or — I just . . . I like to touch it, you
know?*

THE HALLWAY. SADIE AND JENNIFER.

SADIE   : Listen honey, I'm 50 years old today,
I'm your mother and I love you but I'm telling
you something sweetheart. You can't go on
like this. I want you to have a normal life.

JENNIFER   : You want me to be skinny!

THE DEN.
KATE IS NOW BEING INTERVIEWED BY MARTINE.

KATE   : *We used to have this big old black
restaurant stove that was always kept warm.
And I remember curling up on that with my
two best friends, which were food and a book,
because I was always lousy with people.
And I remember that being such a comforting
feeling . . . It wasn't until later when I made the
mistake of thinking that food was the answer to
all of my needs, that it would compensate for my
loneliness, my fears, and my lack of love . . .
It was my only way to control my life. My
parents were very strict and it was the only way
that I had to say this is my body, and I'll do
whatever the hell I want with it.*

THE HALLWAY. SADIE AND JENNIFER.

JENNIFER   : You're representing these people, they're just
                  going to dump you when they get big anyway.

SADIE   : It doesn't matter.

JENNIFER   : I'm going to be a star. I'm going to be a
                  star . . . and without you.

SADIE   : Sweetheart, you don't *need* to be a star.
                  It's the *last* thing in the world you need.

JENNIFER   : Yes, I *do* need to be a star.

SADIE   : You need to be a *human being* who gets
                  married and has children and dresses up for her
                  mother's 50th birthday party.

JENNIFER   : What a bore. What a damned bore.

THE DEN. SOPHIE WALKS IN ON THE INTERVIEWING.

SOPHIE   : What's going on here?

HELENE   : Well, Martine is giving us an interview.

MARTINE   : (Disappointed) Oh no, it was so good.

SOPHIE   : I want to do one.

HELENE   : Oh, please, take my place. I have to go
                  check on people. (She exits)

MARTINE   : Anyway, I haven't finished with Kate yet.
                  (She points camera at Kate)

SOPHIE

: No, no, it's *my* turn. Let *me* do it. She's — (To Kate) Haven't you already *done* one?

KATE

: Well, we — we sort of had a start.

MARTINE

: No, no, no — I have a few other questions . . . don't go . . .

KATE

: (Gets up) Listen. Do Sophie, and I'll be around, you can do me later, okay? (She kisses Martine and exits)

MARTINE

: Thank you . . .

SOPHIE

: She's very generous.

MARTINE

: (Reluctantly, pointing camera at Sophie) Okay, now. What do you want to tell me?

SOPHIE

: I'm a little nervous. I've never done this before.

MARTINE

: Okay, just relax and answer a few questions. Do *you* have any problems?

SOPHIE

: How do I look?

MARTINE

: Do you have any problem with *food*?

SOPHIE

: (Into camera) *No . . . Well, I don't have a problem with food. I have a problem with sugar . . . I mean I've never overeaten a vegetable in my life . . .*

CLOSE-UP. MARTINE, INTERVIEWING.

MARTINE : Do you remember anything about specific foods?

INTERVIEW CLOSE-UPS.
EACH WOMAN IS LOOKING DIRECTLY INTO THE CAMERA.

JENNIFER : *Oatmeal.*

LYDIA : *Sugar Smacks.*

MRS. WILLIAMS : *Caviar. Oh, it's — it's so special.*

SOPHIE : *Chocolate-chip cookies.*

CORY : *Hamilton's Canadian Bacon.*

HELENE : *Zabar's Raisin Pumpernickel Bread.*

CORY : *For years, I would eat it <u>raw</u> . . .*

HELENE : *I'd peel off the crust, which I would eat, very carefully . . .*

CORY : *There was something about the salt. And the greasy kind of oily texture, of the fat. And once, you know, it would almost be gone and the meat would still be left and there would be just this — this sense of <u>fat</u> . . .*

HELENE : *. . . And then I would burrow in the little holes and get the raisins, each little raisin was coated with sort of a sugar coating.*

CORY : *. . . Just the most incredible, sensual sense of fat, with a little bit of rind, just the teeniest bit of rind left.*

KATE : *I have a memory of, on Sunday evenings, watching old, old movies with my mother and we'd sit and cuddle and have a quart of milk and a five-pound box of Sees Candies, that we'd eat. And we'd eat the <u>whole</u> box.*

WALLI : *I like Italian food and men together.*

ELOISE : *Black-eyed peas and mashed potatoes and corn on the cob and butter . . .*

JACKIE : *Grapes!*

ELOISE : *. . . Gravy and biscuits and fried chicken and English peas and fruit cocktail . . .*

GABBY : *Half a gallon of coffee ice cream.*

GERRI : *Brussel sprouts.*

LEE : *Chocolate-chip cookies.*

BEA : *You know that white bread, that cheap white bread . . . And you'd put it in the broiler and the butter would melt and it would get crispy on the outside and it was so good and so warm . . .*

MARIA : *Well, I'm really not involved with food anymore, you know. I found a lot of distractions.*

MARTINE : Like what?

MARIE : *Clothes . . . Men . . . Accessories . . .*

MARTINE : Tell me about your childhood and food.

SADIE : *Oh childhood was great. My papa was there . . .*

GERRI : I *have wonderful memories of childhood because my grandmother, she baked bread twice a week. And — and I love that — that smell, that yeast and — and bread fermenting.*

SADIE : *. . . He used to sit me on his lap and he'd love to watch me eat. And my mama loved to watch me eat. And — and they loved to cook for me . . .*

MILLIE : *First day of school, private school, the teacher was standing there with a donut . . .* (She laughs)

SADIE : *. . . It was <u>wonderful</u>! . . .*

MILLIE : *. . . And I just went over and stood by the teacher and just ate it right out of her hand, you know, while it was hanging down there. And all she had left was this little piece in her hand, you know? And I spent my first day of school in the corner, 'cause I ate the teacher's donut.*

SADIE : *. . . And somewhere along the line, I got to feeling like every time I wanted to feel <u>wonderful</u> and when life disappointed me, I thought, "Well I'll eat something, and then I'll feel wonderful again." Except, you know, I got fat.* (She laughs)

CECE : *When I was two and a half years old, my sister was born. Up until that time, I was the apple of my father's eye.*

MARIA : *The first thing I can remember is pleasing my father, and eating a lot. And then he turned on me, and told me I was a bull in a china shop and a lummox . . .*

CECE : *. . . It's not that he didn't love me, it's just that he thought I was ugly . . . and he let me know it.*

MARIA : . . . *I'm not a bull in a china shop.*

GABBY : *I found a letter from my mother . . . when I was two months old she wrote a letter to my grandmother, saying that I ate like a pig.*

CATHY : *My mother drank about a six pack of Coca-Colas every day. I had Coca-Cola in my baby bottle and — I'm from the South, and that's what you did — you just gave your kid sugar . . .*

ANITA : *These cakes that were brought in today, I mean they sort of epitomize my memories of childhood . . .*

CATHY : *. . . And that sugar was sweet. And that sweetness was something I became very addicted to, 'cause I didn't have that in my life . . .*

ANITA : *. . . A big to-do about celebrating my birthday and all the people and the gifts and stuff, and then this — this great sense of loneliness . . .*

CATHY : *. . . Just the wanting to connect with something. It just made me feel connected. For very fleeting moments, but during that time I was eating, I felt connected . . .*

ANITA : *. . . I think it was just food and me, you know, as a kid. I . . . I think I was left alone a lot . . . I think. And I was left alone with food . . . And it was very comforting.*

CATHY : (Tears welling up in her eyes) *I'm never going to ever be able to be like normal people with food. I mean, I'm always going to be at the mercy of it. And it's a very, very scary feeling. It's very, very powerful. And I hate it. And — and, uh, and yet, uh, I can't stop. And I can't live without it . . . And that's torturous . . .*

OUTSIDE IN THE GARDEN, AT A TABLE. MARTINE IS SITTING
ALONE, THINKING ABOUT THE INTERVIEWS SHE HAS JUST
FILMED. HELENE COMES OUT OF THE HOUSE AND JOINS HER.

HELENE   : Martine.

MARTINE   : Hi.

HELENE   : Hi. I brought you this. (She hands her a
                glass of champagne)

MARTINE   : (She takes the glass) Thank you.

HELENE   : (She sits down opposite Martine)
                So. How's it going?

MARTINE   : I think it's wonderful. The party's going very
                well. Don't you think?

HELENE   : The party's great, isn't it? Yes — But your
                filming. How are you feeling about it?

MARTINE   : Well, I'm just amazed. I mean, I've got some
                — such amazing things.

HELENE   : Yeah?

MARTINE   : But, your friends are wonderful, I think.

HELENE   : They are . . . They're really great.

MARTINE   : Happy birthday. (She toasts her. They clink
                glasses)

HELENE   : Thank you. (They drink)

THE DEN. SOPHIE IS ON THE PHONE.

SOPHIE : Doctor Lorenz? Hi, it's Sophie. I — I know, I'm sorry. I just — I'm at this party and I — I think I'm in trouble here. And you told me to call you whenever I think that — that there's going to be a problem . . .

THE GARDEN TABLE. HELENE AND MARTINE.

HELENE : Why aren't you filming?

MARTINE : Well I just stopped for a while, you know? I've heard a lot of things . . . I was just thinking . . .

HELENE : Yeah?

MARTINE : Yeah.

HELENE : You look, uh —

MARTINE : I look what?

HELENE : Well no, you just looked upset for a moment.

MARTINE : I'm not upset, no. I'm just — a little, you know — there's been a lot going on.

KATE WALKS OUT OF THE HOUSE,
AND JOINS THEM AT THE TABLE.

KATE : Hi.

MARTINE : Hi.

HELENE : Hi, Kate.

KATE   : It's too crazy in there for me.

HELENE   : Is it?

MARTINE   : Yes, it is. (She smiles)

KATE   : You're taking a break? You're not going to film for a while?

MARTINE   : Mm hmm. It gets a little too emotional sometimes, this thing. But I hope you don't mind my doing this. I mean it's just so interesting for me, you know, to catch those — those things . . .

HELENE   : I think it's great.

MARTINE   :   To tell you the truth, my whole documentary is about that: *Women and food.* That's really why I'm here for.

HELENE   : Really?

MARTINE   : Yeah.

HELENE   : Why then did you say the documentary was about women in California?

MARTINE   : Well I said "Southern Californian Behavior" because it's more general. You know, it seems awkward to people when you say "women and food." They just start wondering why "women and food?" . . . You know we don't talk about these things in France. The first time I heard *bulimia* was about Jane Fonda, when she said that — but we don't discuss that, at all. So I felt so *alone* . . .

MARY   : Did *you* throw up?

MARTINE : Well yes . . . The first time I threw up, actually, I was thinking I was doing something real smart. I remember it was with a friend, and it was like a very good idea. You eat, so then you throw up. It was very, you know, a very smart idea. I didn't know it was going to lead to all these terrible things . . . The doctors said, well, a lot of women do that to control their weight and that's okay, and it was nothing to worry about.

HELENE : You know, 20 or 30 years ago, I think sex was the secret subject of women . . . And now it's food . . .

MARTINE : It's such a — unattractive —

HELENE : I know, it makes you feel awful, doesn't it?

MARTINE : It's terrible. It's the most terrible thing. You know you can say, "I'm an alcoholic," I feel, or "I'm a drug addict," that's okay. It's, you know, kind of *interesting*. But just say, "I have an eating disorder, I just want to *eat*, I just want . . ." that's so unattractive, it's so *disturbing* . . . and I was never able to tell that to *anyone*.

HELENE : The other night I found this whole empty quart of ice cream by my bed. I could not believe it. I had walked in my sleep. I couldn't believe I'd done it.

KATE : And you didn't remember?

HELENE : I did not remember.

MARTINE : Oh yes, that's happened to me.

HELENE   : It was like black-out. It was the most — has
                that happened to *you*?

MARTINE   : Yeah.

HELENE   : It *has*?

MARTINE   : You know, that I wake up and I realize I've been
                eating during the night . . . I don't know . . .

HELENE   : Martine. You're upset.

MARTINE   : I'm sorry . . . It's just listening to these
                women, I — I didn't think it would get so much
                stuff out of me . . .

THE DEN. SOPHIE IS STILL ON THE PHONE.

SOPHIE   : I don't . . . well do you think I should talk to
                somebody here? But you see, I'm afraid if I talk
                to somebody, that I'm . . . I'm afraid I'm going
                to do something *vicious* . . .

A BEDROOM. JENNIFER AND ANITA ARE SITTING ON THE BED.
JENNIFER IS EATING ANOTHER SLICE OF CAKE.

JENNIFER   : My mother doesn't understand that it's okay
                to eat.

ANITA   : Well, as a mother, I mean, I would say you can
                eat. I don't know about eating *that*, though.

JENNIFER   : I mean . . . this is like *Mozart* !

ANITA   : That's a lot of carbohydrates . . . *Mozart* ?

JENNIFER   : Yeah, I think food is like music.

THE DEN. SOPHIE ON THE PHONE.

SOPHIE : I'm calming down a little . . . Yeah, but I
don't know if I can do this if you're not on the
phone with me . . .

THE DINING ROOM. ELOISE AND LEE
(A YOUNG MODEL/ACTRESS) ARE AT A TABLE.

LEE : I think you're an incredible actress and I
know you just have it all together and you don't
have any problems and I just want to *be* you . . .
I colored my hair like yours. (She laughs)

ELOISE : (Bemused) You just want to be me.

THE BEDROOM. JENNIFER AND ANITA ON THE BED.

JENNIFER : . . . You know, Beethoven is *beef* . . .
Stravinski, *salad*, you know, mixed salad, with
pickles. Vivaldi's *fruit* . . . fruit salad . . . A big
bowl of fruit . . .

ANITA : (Points at Jennifer's cake) What's *that*? . . .
That's Tchaikovsky, that's *tragic*! (They laugh)

THE DINING ROOM. ELOISE AND LEE.

LEE : I want to just ask you a few things, 'cause you
know so much.

ELOISE : Yeah.

LEE : Do I have to sleep with someone in order to
get a part?

ELOISE : How *big* a part?

THE PHONE RINGS.
SOPHIE IS STANDING IN A CORNER, ALONE,
MUNCHING ON A BIG YELLOW PEPPER.
SHE SEES HELENE IN THE DEN.
HELENE ANSWERS THE PHONE.

HELENE   : Hello? . . . Oh, Frank?

THE LIVING ROOM. KATE AND MRS. WILLIAMS ARE ON A SOFA.

KATE   : What's it like being married as long as you were?

MRS. WILLIAMS : Well, in many ways it was wonderful . . .
                I guess *most* of it was wonderful . . . The only
                thing is, I was married when I was *so* young, I
                feel like I was married for three-quarters of my
                life. My late husband wasn't that much in
                accord of my career, because I was a singer at
                the time we were married, so there were some
                regrets about *that* . . . And yet again, he was so
                terrific that, it's good . . . Or it *was* good . . .

THE DEN. HELENE IS ON THE PHONE.
SOPHIE IS SECRETLY LISTENING
AND CHEWING ON HER PEPPER WITH A VENGEANCE.

HELENE : What do you *mean* you can't come home
tonight, darling? Bernard changed the
reservations, specially . . . I want my husband
on my birthday . . . Is that so much to ask?
You should be happy that I love you so much
. . . Alright . . . Okay . . . It's just that I've got all
these presents here and *you're* the one I really
want . . . Alright, I mean I'm fine, I'm just fine,
I just miss you that's all . . . Okay, tomorrow . . .
Yes, darling, I understand . . . Bye . . .

THE LIVING ROOM.
KATE AND MRS. WILLIAMS ON THE SOFA.

MRS. WILLIAMS : . . . I lived with my mother until I was 18,
I went to New York, then I moved in with a girl
in New York when I was modeling, and then I
got married . . . in other words, I sort of lost
track of *me* along the way. But you don't seem
to have done that.

KATE : I don't know. I guess maybe that's one of
my questions, you know? Because I haven't
been alone and so I don't really know if the me
that I think is me has to do with my Prince
Charming on the hill and my horses and that
life, or if it's something else that I just haven't
explored. You know?

MRS. WILLIAMS : If you have what you *seem* to have, I'd give a
lot of thought to try to squelch some antsy,
reckless or restless feelings . . .

CLOSE-UP INTERVIEWS, ONE AFTER THE OTHER.
EACH WOMAN LOOKS DIRECTLY INTO THE CAMERA.

JANICE   : *I like to __eat__ . . . I like to eat food . . . I like to
                have dinner . . . I don't like to skip meals . . .
                I don't like to fast.*

GERRI   : *I've always loved to eat.*

LESLIE   : *I love eating. I was born to eat.*

LEE   : *I've thought about moving to Europe several
                times . . . I would go to Italy and I would be this
                __zoftig__ woman that the men would love and I
                could eat whatever I wanted and dive into
                bowls of spaghetti . . .*

BERRY   : *I want the people that are important to me in
                my life to love me whether my fanny is perfect or
                my thighs are perfect or whether when I wave
                goodbye, my arm shakes . . .*

LESLIE   : *Nobody __had__ eating problems when I was
                growing up. My mother didn't. I didn't know
                anybody who had eating problems, you know,
                so it's just not part of my vocabulary.*

JANICE   : *I think I'm overweight because I look in
                magazines and I see, you know, people with __no__
                bodies. Like, when I wake up in the morning,
                I don't feel like, oh, I'm so fat. But when I turn
                on the TV or if I look at ads in Vogue, I'll see the
                Bain de Soleil woman and I'll __think__, "I better get
                to the gym . . ."*

THE LIVING ROOM. SOPHIE, ON A COUCH, ALONE IN
THE ROOM, IS CALMING HERSELF, PATTING HER CHEST
GENTLY, WHISPERING TO HERSELF REASSURINGLY.

SOPHIE : It's okay . . . Everything's alright . . .We look
great today . . . We look great . . . Just a group
of women . . . It's okay . . .

THE DEN. MRS. WILLIAMS IS IN A LARGE CHAIR.
HELENE IS SITTING ON THE ARM.

MRS. WILLIAMS : How long has this gone on?

HELENE : I don't really know. You know, he calls and
says he has to work late at the office . . .
And then, of course, I have to get up early . . .
I feel I never *see* him . . . I don't know . . .
I *just* don't know . . . All I know is he's
spending nights out, late . . . I *just* don't know,
mom . . . I just don't know . . . Maybe he can't
face the fact that I'm getting old . . .

MRS. WILLIAMS : Oh, come on . . .

HELENE : Maybe *I* can't face the fact.

MRS. WILLIAMS : If *you* say that, what do you think that makes
me feel like?

HELENE : Oh, mom . . .

MRS. WILLIAMS : . . . A *dinosaur* . . . (She laughs)

HELENE : It's going to be okay, isn't it mom?

MRS. WILLIAMS : Of course it is.

HELENE : Of course it's going to be okay.

TWO INTERVIEWS:
BEA AND ELOISE, INTERCUT WITH ONE ANOTHER.

BEA : *Food is the only thing that I can count on, for unconditional love. Food is the only thing that will comfort me and love me and be good to me and sweet to me 24 hours a day. I can go into the kitchen, I can open the refrigerator and I can have a muffin with jelly or whatever I want on it, and it makes me feel good and gives me love . . .*

ELOISE : *I think that there only have been two things that have ever really interested me, and that's food and men . . .*

BEA : *The only man who has ever loved me unconditionally was my grandfather . . .*

ELOISE : *If the food doesn't work, then I go to men. So I'm either hungry or in love . . .*

BEA : *. . . He would hold me in his arms and he would sing "Old Time Religion," you know, "Give Me That Old Time Religion." And that is the last man that has ever loved me unconditionally.*

ELOISE : *I think I'm still looking for a man who could excite me as much as a baked potato!*

THE GARDEN. HELENE AND SOPHIE AT A TABLE.

HELENE : Do you know anything that's going on that I don't know? (She is picking at a roll of bread)

SOPHIE : What do you mean, what's going on?

HELENE : I don't know, I just have this *feeling*. I just have this kind of psychic feeling that something's not right with Frank. And I — I don't know what it is. I mean I don't want to be paranoid about it, but something doesn't *feel* right.

SOPHIE : Are you at this point in your life where you absolutely don't trust your feelings?

HELENE : Yes, I don't trust my feelings. I don't *want* to trust my feelings. (She eats the roll)

SOPHIE : Well, what is going on is that there is this terrible conspiracy of silence. And I'm sick of it and I'm angry about it. *Everyone* knows at the party about it, except you. And I don't believe that *you* don't know.

HELENE : What does *that* mean?

SOPHIE : Frank is having an affair.

HELENE : That's not true . . . that's not true . . .

SOPHIE : Helene, I hate telling you this. I just, oh, I just *hate* it. I don't want to hurt you any more than you're already hurt.

HELENE : Just because he's called me three times, because he doesn't . . . Just because he's called me and just 'cause I have a feeling inside? . . . Just because he's not coming home for my birthday? . . . Maybe it's just from — from something else . . . Maybe it's just from my own craziness . . .

SOPHIE : Helene —

HELENE : I'm sorry I asked you out here.

SOPHIE   : No, Helene —

HELENE   : I'm sorry, I thought you were my friend. I really thought you were my best friend. (She gets up to leave)

SOPHIE   : *Sit down* and *deal* with this . . . Just sit down! . . . Okay, just calm down please . . . Would you just calm down . . . I mean look at all this food — this eating, I mean you've been eating non-stop since I got here.

HELENE   : I've been eating . . . you're making me eat.

SOPHIE   : No, you're —

HELENE   : You *are* making me *eat*!

SOPHIE   : No, Helene —

HELENE   : You're making me eat. You're making me *sick*!

SOPHIE   : He's having an affair with someone here.

HELENE   : Somebody here?

SOPHIE   : Someone here. And the woman —

HELENE   : Somebody here?

SOPHIE   : The woman's a brunette . . . I don't know for sure if she's a brunette, but this is — this is what I think, this is what I —

HELENE   : How do you know?

SOPHIE   : I've *heard* it.

HELENE   : What do you mean you've heard it?

SOPHIE   : I've heard that he's having an affair with a brunette at the party.

HELENE   : Who did you hear it from? Where did you get your information?

SOPHIE   : I'm not going to get into something *gossipy* with you.

HELENE   : Sophie, *please.*

SOPHIE   : Oh, Helene, you *have* this information.

HELENE   : Don't do this to me. Tell me who it *is.*

SOPHIE   : It's a brunette . . . That's all I heard . . . You can deal with this . . .

HELENE   : Okay . . . A brunette? A brunette . . . Half the people at the party are brunette.

SOPHIE   : Go and find out who it is and *confront* her! Get in touch with your rage and *deal* with this!

MARTINE BEHIND THE CAMERA.

MARTINE   : What about sex?

CLOSE-UP INTERVIEWS, ONE AFTER ANOTHER.

GABBY   : *I can't have sex after I eat.*

MILLIE   : *I have to be thin to have sex.*

MARIA   : *Well, I always feel better when I have sex.*

GABBY   : *I have to have sex before I eat, because if I have sex after I eat, I feel fat. And I don't want to be touched when I feel fat . . .*

CHRIS   : *Black men love hips . . .*

GABBY   : *. . . Of course this used to drive my boyfriends crazy . . .*

CHRIS   : *. . . When I'm with a black man, the more the merrier, you know what I mean? And when you're with a white man, the American white man, they don't particularly like a whole lot on a woman's hips . . .*

GABBY   : *. . . I'd want to make love earlier and they'd want to make love later, and I would never tell them . . .*

CHRIS   : *. . . I found that I had shaped myself to whoever I was going with, you know?*

RUTH   : *My childhood and everything was pretty sexual . . .*

GABBY   : *. . . I wouldn't say I can't make love after dinner, that sounds ridiculous . . .*

RUTH : *. . . Always thinking about sex, sexual fantasies and everything . . .*

GABBY : *. . . I just used to try and make love earlier and then we'd end up eating dinner anyway, 'cause I wouldn't tell them . . .*

RUTH : *. . . In my twenties, going into my thirties, maybe 80 percent of my time and energy was about food, diets, being thin . . .*

GABBY : *. . . And then we'd go to bed and I didn't want to make love. 'Cause I felt fat!*

RUTH : *. . . I found myself having a sexual relationship a couple of times when I didn't want to be there and I didn't want to be having sex. And at the time it didn't occur to me that I had the option to say no . . .*

ANITA : *I think about sex and food often . . .*

RUTH : *. . . And I began to eat . . .*

ANITA : *. . . I had a lot of Catholic influences when I was little . . .*

RUTH : *. . . All I could think about was what I could eat, where could I eat it and when could I eat it . . .*

ANITA : *. . . I still relate to food very much pertaining to the child in me, and sex is belonging to that adult in me . . .*

RUTH : *. . . I loved that I was getting fat . . .*

ANITA : *. . . Eating and being good, that's okay . . .*

RUTH : *. . . I got very unsexual . . .*

ANITA   : . . . *Sex, I have to talk myself into that it's*
                 actually okay . . . And then it's — then it's okay!
                 (She laughs)

RUTH   : . . . *I made myself <u>unattractive</u> enough that*
                 men didn't approach me anymore . . . So I could
                 never be in that situation . . . I was safe!

THE KITCHEN. HELENE IS ALONE, CRYING.
SHE PICKS UP A STRAWBERRY, EATS IT, AND CRIES SOME MORE.

HELENE   : You . . . bastard! (She picks up another strawberry)

THE STAIRCASE. MARTINE IS TRYING TO INTERVIEW THE
TWO COOKS, WHO DECLINE.

MARTINE   : I would like to ask you a few questions on
                 camera, if you don't mind.

CONNIE   : No, I — I can't — no — I'd feel uncomfortable
                 about it . . .

NAOMI   : We can't really talk about — what we were
                 talking about . . .

THE BATHROOM. THE DOOR OPENS AND MRS. WILLIAMS
GENTLY PULLS HELENE INSIDE, THEN CLOSES THE DOOR
FROM WITHIN, SHUTTING OUT THE PARTY NOISES.

HELENE   : Why are you bringing me up here, mother?
                 You can't do that. I have a party going on . . .

MRS. WILLIAMS : I know you do. There are so many people
                 walking around talking —

HELENE   : Oh, mother, why are you smoking?

MRS. WILLIAMS : Oh, come on —

HELENE : Darling, you've *got* to put your cigarette out . . . I won't have it. (She puts it out)

MRS. WILLIAMS : Well, you're being a *bore.*

HELENE : Mother, it's not good for you.

MRS. WILLIAMS : *That's* not good for me? *This* is not good for you. (Indicating drink) You have had so much to drink and it's early in the evening.

HELENE : I know. I know.

MRS. WILLIAMS : Helene, what is *wrong?*

HELENE : I think that, uh, Frank is having an affair and it's the one thing I really can't stand — I won't stand for it.

MRS. WILLIAMS : Men are just basically that way, they get bored — you know the cliché, "Familiarity breeds contempt?" It takes a lot for two people to stay together. And anywhere near happiness, I mean, that's a *miracle.* But if you are smart, you love Frank, you want to hold on to him, *don't* do this. *Don't* just close the door now. Don't make up your mind of that. Please try to make up your mind that you're going to hang in there . . . That's the way *we* did it . . . We turned our backs or we accepted it. And went on . . . And everything worked out just fine. You want to be alone the rest of your life?

HELENE : No.

MRS. WILLIAMS : It's not easy out there today. There are so *many* attractive, young, beautiful, successful, talented, brilliant women . . . You want to take that chance?

HELENE   : Mother, I know. But I can't put up with this.
                This is a trust that's been broken. I cannot put
                up with this. I cannot *hide* anymore. I am too
                old to hide. I don't want to do it. I've hidden
                half of my life, mother. I must face the truth.
                I've got to *face* it.

MRS. WILLIAMS : It seems like you have made more of a
                mess of your lives today than we *ever* did.
                You will regret this for the rest of your life.
                You've got to compromise, you've got to be
                understanding . . . It wasn't that easy with your
                father, but fortunately *my* mother was wise
                enough to tell me to hang in there, turn my
                back, ignore it . . . It's just a natural trait of the
                male animal.

HELENE   : Oh, mother . . . I do love you, mother . . .
                I truly wish I could do what you did . . .
                But I just can't. I can't do it.

THE KITCHEN. SOPHIE AND MARTINE.

SOPHIE   : What do you think about Frank?

MARTINE   : Frank?

SOPHIE : Mmhmm. Helene's husband?

MARTINE : I like him. Why?

SOPHIE : He's attractive, no?

MARTINE : Well, yes, I suppose so. I mean, I like him. He's my father's best friend, you know.

SOPHIE : Is he?

MARTINE : Yeah.

A COUCH. MARIA AND JACKIE.

MARIA : (Smoking her cigarette) I started eating ice cream, you know, with the modeling . . . And of course, I blew up . . . And *then* I got into drugs, which was wonderful, you know, until drugs stopped working . . . And *then* we went into men . . . But then I have this thing for Jewish men and also Jewish men who don't smoke . . . So we're into a *real* problem with that, you know . . . So I, every four months, I start smoking again. I get four months *in* and then, you know, I get a break-up. And I go into *grief* and then I'm thin again . . . I break up relationships so that I can smoke!

THE KITCHEN. SOPHIE AND MARTINE.

SOPHIE : He's very charming isn't he?

MARTINE : Yeah.

SOPHIE : And attractive?

MARTINE : Well, he *is*.

SOPHIE   : Do you think he's sexy?

MARTINE   : (Laughs) Oh my God, you're so obsessed.
                  Yes, I suppose so, yes, of course he's sexy.

SOPHIE   : He *is*, isn't he?

MARTINE   : Yeah.

THE STAIRCASE. HELENE AND LYDIA ARE SITTING ON IT.

HELENE   : My darling, you know, when I married your
                  father, you were nine years old.

LYDIA   : I know.

HELENE   : And I fell in love with you then, just like you
                  were my own little girl.

LYDIA   : Well, you know I love you like a mom.

HELENE   : I still feel the same way about you.

LYDIA   : Yeah.

HELENE   : No matter what happens. No matter what
                  happens, no matter where *any*one goes, I will
                  always love you.

LYDIA   : What does *that* mean?

THE COUCH. JACKIE AND MARIA.

JACKIE   : I've been doing pretty good about my food.
                  You know, if I just don't eat until around . . .
                  eleven at night, I'm alright. If I eat — if I start
                  eating earlier, I just — I just keep eating and
                  eating and eating, and I can't stop.
                  (Maria nods, understandingly)

THE KITCHEN. SOPHIE AND MARTINE.

SOPHIE : Do you like older men? Why are you embarrassed?

MARTINE : I'm *not* embarrassed.

SOPHIE : You *are*, look at you, you put your head down — yes, you are. Why are you embarrassed?

MARTINE : Well, I like older men, yes.

SOPHIE : You do?

MARTINE : I just wondered how it showed.

SOPHIE : Because of your reaction when I asked you. I mean, I'm not blind.

MARTINE : How did you get this idea? Yes, I do.

SOPHIE : I didn't. I just was curious.

MARTINE : I do. I do like older men.

SOPHIE : Do you only *go* with older men?

MARTINE : Most of the time.

SOPHIE : I like older men, too.

MARTINE : They're so comfortable, aren't they?

SOPHIE : *Very* comfortable. (They both laugh)

THE COUCH. MARIA AND JACKIE.

MARIA   : You know how *I* did it. When I stopped
                 those drugs, it was just so traumatic that I got
                 on my knees and I told God that I'll do *anything*
                 if He doesn't strike me fat. (They laugh) And
                 it's *worked*!

JACKIE   : Only you would talk to Him that way, though.

MARIA   : Oh, honey.

THE DEN. KATE AND HELENE ON A COUCH.
HELENE IS EATING A SLICE OF CAKE WITH HER FINGERS.
SHE LOOKS SUSPICIOUSLY AT KATE.

KATE   : What?

HELENE   : Do you have anything to tell me?

KATE   : Yeah, you're eating too much cake. Got it on
                 your face. (She picks it off)

HELENE   : You don't have anything *else* to tell me?

KATE   : No . . . Now would you cool it on the cake?

TWO INTERVIEWS: CECE AND GERRI.

CECE   : *Secretly, in my dreams, I go to bed every night*
                 and I dream about waking up and looking in
                 the mirror and being Ann-Margaret.

GERRI   : *. . . When it came to dessert, I thought, "Well,*
                 I'm not going to have dessert," I mean, you
                 know, not for the first date. I mean I've got to
                 show some restraint . . .

CECE : *Some girls have husbands and boyfriends and lovers and employers and houses and I have rye bread and cream cheese.*

GERRI : *. . . But he insisted that I have dessert if I really wanted it, and I said "Well I really do want it" and he said, "Have dessert" . . . So we both had dessert . . .*

CECE : *I've lost 50 pounds ten times in the last eight years.*

GERRI : *. . . It's not a reward. It's just if I want dessert, I have dessert. Because it's a normal thing to have dessert if you want dessert . . .*

CECE : *I want a guy who's going to like me for what I am and who I am. And the fact that I have a little mileage, you know . . . it's okay.*

GERRI : *. . . And then he said, "Would you like another dessert?" And I said, "Well, no, I guess I really don't want another dessert. One dessert was good. That's fine." But the fact that he offered me another dessert and it was okay, oh I was just . . . oh, it was just really good!*

THE DEN. ON THE FLOOR, BY THE FIREPLACE, SIT MARTINE AND HELENE, EATING ASPARAGUS. HELENE IS LOOKING SUSPICIOUSLY AT MARTINE.

MARTINE : It's a wonderful party . . . I think my documentary is going to be terrific.

HELENE : Yeah?

MARTINE : I've got all these great interviews.

HELENE   : You have nothing to say about Frank?

MARTINE   : No, why?

HELENE   : Just curious . . . Just curious . . .

MARTINE   : Is there something wrong? Can I help?

HELENE   : Is there nothing you want to tell me?

MARTINE   : I have hardly seen Frank the past few days.
                  He is never at home.

HELENE   : He comes home late. You stay up late. I go
                  to bed early.

MARTINE   : I know, I may have met him a few times, you
                  know, just have a few — had a few talks. Are
                  you sure you're okay? I like you. I really do.
                  (She smiles at Helene, finishing her asparagus)

KATE, ON THE KITCHEN PHONE.

KATE   : Hey, baby. Oh God, I miss you . . .
                  I just wish I were home . . .

INTERVIEWS, DIRECTLY INTO THE CAMERA.

NANCY   : *Oh God. Is there any particular reason why
                  you want to ask me about food? Is it because
                  you think I'm fat?*

MRS. WILLIAMS   : *Food, food, food. That's all I hear is food.
                  Now I really enjoy eating, I always have. But in
                  my time, we'd get together to have a drink. Oh,
                  cocktails and hors d'oeuvres, I mean that was
                  always — you know, that was a more desirable
                  invitation than going to dinner.*

KATE ON THE PHONE.

KATE   : . . . No. I just — I just wanted to send you a hug and tell you that I miss you. I just wish I was home, hiding in your arms . . .

THE DEN. MRS. WILLIAMS' INTERVIEW CONTINUES.

MRS. WILLIAMS : *I don't think Helene ever really <u>had</u> a problem with food. I mean as a child. There was no, uh, — certainly no obsession with it. She liked food, but she wasn't even that crazy about it. Well maybe I'm just mid-Victorian, Southern. I just can't understand this craving — this obsession with <u>food</u>. I wish I did.*

HELENE, WHO HAS BEEN SITTING AND LISTENING IN THE BACKGROUND, WALKS UP TO HER MOTHER AND KNEELS BY HER CHAIR.

HELENE   : Oh, mother.

MRS. WILLIAMS : I don't know what I'm saying here . . .

HELENE   : I know.

MRS. WILLIAMS : . . . Or why she particularly wants this on film. (To Martine) Could — could you please — let's not do this anymore . . . Thank you . . .

KATE ON THE PHONE.

KATE   : . . . Well, okay . . . Okay, get back to that . . . I just wanted to say that I love you . . .

NANCY'S INTERVIEW.

NANCY   : . . . *I can just remember in girl's school, that was all we did, was eat. I mean it was just company, it was the best thing in the world. It's just that my metabolism can't take it. I just get really huge and I have weighed as much as 200 pounds in my life. And I think that once you are that heavy, it's very hard for you to ever really feel thin* . . .

THE DEN. HELENE AND HER MOTHER, ALONE NOW.

HELENE   : I guess you never knew that I had a problem with food . . . That's what's so funny . . .You see, you always *said* I never had a problem. You always said I never had a problem.

MRS. WILLIAMS : But you *didn't.*

HELENE   : Mother!

MRS. WILLIAMS : When did this start? When you say "always," what do you mean by "always?"

HELENE : Well, not always, but when Nancy was born. You don't remember that I ate myself sick? That I had to play a *pumpkin* because I was too fat to be anything else? You don't *remember* that?

MRS. WILLIAMS : Oh, you were never really fat. You —

HELENE : I know, that's what you always *said*.

NANCY'S INTERVIEW.
NANCY : . . . *I wear clothes to conceal it. I mean I have this jacket on because I don't want you to see my fat arms* . . .

THE DEN. HELENE AND HER MOTHER.

HELENE : Not long ago, I took an LSD trip. And I threw up for eight hours straight, and you know what?

MRS. WILLIAMS : (Shaken, apprehensive) No.

HELENE : I finally threw up Nancy.

MRS. WILLIAMS : . . . Oh, my God. I just can't —

HELENE : I know . . .

MRS. WILLIAMS : I just *can't* — I can't under*stand* this . . . I just can't *fathom* it . . .

HELENE : I know, it's hard . . . It's *my* problem, too. I'm not blaming you. I'm just saying it's something I couldn't talk to you about.

MRS. WILLIAMS : Does that mean I was so unaware? . . .

NANCY'S INTERVIEW.

NANCY   : . . . *Men think that I'm crazy because I'm*
                 obsessed with my weight. And that I am always
                 very particular about what I eat . . .

THE DEN. HELENE AND HER MOTHER.

MRS. WILLIAMS : . . . And so insensitive to you?

HELENE   : No, I was so secret . . .

NANCY'S INTERVIEW.

NANCY   : . . . *Every time that I open the refrigerator,*
                 I think, "What? Are you going to eat? You're not
                 going to eat again, are you? You better be
                 careful . . . Are you eating that much??"

THE DEN. HELENE LOOKS AT HER MOTHER,
WHO IS DEEP IN THOUGHT.

THE LIVING ROOM. NANCY SIGHS, HER INTERVIEW OVER.

THE DINING ROOM.
SOPHIE AND BEA ARE SITTING BY THE TABLE.

BEA   : I'm so uncomfortable being here.

SOPHIE   : What are you angry about?

BEA   : Oh, Helene's husband, Frank. You know,
                 Frank? Oh, he drives me crazy. I had an affair
                 with him years ago. It wasn't even an affair.
                 He fucked me and left me. He didn't even fuck
                 me. I mean he just kind of *left* me . . .

JENNIFER, IN THE GARDEN ALONE AT A TABLE,
SECRETLY EATING ANOTHER SLICE OF CAKE.

THE DINING ROOM. SOPHIE AND BEA CONTINUE.

SOPHIE   : Wait a minute. When was this? When *was*
                this?

BEA   : Can you believe it? That was about 15 years
                ago.

SOPHIE   : Fifteen years ago, he was a therapist, and you
                fucked Frank and then he left you?

BEA   : I fucked Frank, and he left me, but he wasn't
                a therapist yet, he was studying to *be* a therapist
                . . . His *father* was a therapist. He was going
                through a really hard time. His father had
                written him this letter about how to be a great
                Gestalt therapist, and he couldn't sleep at night,
                he had mattresses on the floor and blankets on
                the windows and he had blinders 'cause he
                couldn't sleep and fans rolling . . . I mean I *had*
                to fuck him, he couldn't sleep!!

TWO INTERVIEWS: ELOISE AND HER SISTER, BERRY.

ELOISE   : *My daddy always wanted my sister and me to
                be real pretty and that meant to be real thin.*

BERRY   : *When you have a mother that has a waist
                that's 21 inches . . .*

ELOISE   : *When we'd sit at the table, he wouldn't let me
                eat, because I always wanted to and he would
                make her eat because she didn't want to. So she
                slipped me bacon under the table.*

BERRY   : *A mother who glides into a room like Loretta Young . . .*

ELOISE   : *She could have anything she wanted because she didn't want anything, but I couldn't have anything that I wanted because I wanted everything.*

BERRY   : *We'd have a Mars Bar at the table and she would cut it in five little pieces . . . Daddy got one, I got one, my sister got one, there was one for mother, and there was always one left over somewhere hidden in a bag in the kitchen . . .*

ELOISE   : *And mother'd make me run around the block two or three times because I'm — I'm high strung.*

BERRY   : *I never found the other piece . . .*

THE LIVING ROOM. ALL THE WOMEN ARE GATHERED
ON COUCHES, CHAIRS, AND ON THE FLOOR.
HELENE SITS AT THE PIANO
AND STANDING NEXT TO HER IS HER MOTHER.

MRS. WILLIAMS : I have a little *extra* birthday present for you.
Do you remember how I used to sing "The Way
You Look Tonight?" Like, a lot? (She laughs)
Okay . . . Let me see . . .

SHE HITS A NOTE ON THE PIANO, THEN SINGS *A CAPPELLA*:

Some day, when I'm awfully low
And the world is cold
I will feel aglow just thinking of you
And the way you look tonight.
Oh, but you're lovely
With your smile so warm
And your cheeks so soft
There is nothing for me but to love you
Just the way you look tonight.
With each smile, your tenderness grows
Tearing my fears apart
And that smile that wrinkles your nose
Touches my foolish heart.
Lovely, never never change
Keep that breathless charm
Won't you please arrange it, 'cause I love you.
Just the way you look tonight.

MRS. WILLIAMS KISSES HER DAUGHTER.
THE WOMEN APPLAUD WARMLY, QUITE MOVED.
TEARS IN SOME EYES AND SOME NOSE-BLOWING.

HELENE   : (To all the women) Shall we make her sing
another one?

ALL THE WOMEN SHOUT, "YES!" AND APPLAUD.

HELENE   : I practiced this especially for you, mom . . .

THE UPSTAIRS BATHROOM. JENNIFER IS ALONE,
SITTING ON THE EDGE OF THE TUB,
EATING YET ANOTHER PIECE OF CAKE.
SOPHIE ENTERS, SITS NEXT TO HER ON THE CLOSED
TOILET SEAT. IN THE BACKGROUND, WE FAINTLY HEAR
THE PIANO AND MRS. WILLIAMS SINGING.

SOPHIE   : Hi . . . What are you doing?

JENNIFER   : Eating.

SOPHIE   : In the bathroom?

JENNIFER   : Oh, I don't like to — to eat in public. I feel
                 kind of uncomfortable swallowing it . . . It's
                 more comfortable here. (She laughs) There's
                 a seat.

SOPHIE   : You binge. Don't you?

JENNIFER   : No, I was just having a piece —

SOPHIE   : Oh come on, I've been binging since I was
                 your age. I know about binging.

JENNIFER   : Please don't tell my mother I'm eating. She'll
                 just go crazy. She's really neurotic about this.
                 All she cares is that I'm skinny. She doesn't
                 care anything about me as long as I'm skinny,
                 'cause she doesn't want me to look bad for her,
                 you know? And it just makes me want to eat
                 more, because she doesn't let me *be* what I
                 want to *be*, you know? Maybe if she would let
                 me be who I *am*, I wouldn't eat so much.

SOPHIE   : No, that's just an excuse.

JENNIFER   : No, it's the truth. She makes me feel so
                 miserable.

SOPHIE : I'm going to tell you something. When I came here today and I saw Martine in the bathing suit, I was so jealous I couldn't stand it. And it just makes me feel like I'm not good enough. And that everyone here is so pretty. They have the perfect body, perfect face, perfect hair, and I'm just — I feel so inadequate.

JENNIFER : Oh, you're crazy.

SOPHIE : But that's how I *feel.* And you don't want to end up like me.

JENNIFER : Every time I see food, I just — I — I *see* it, it's like the only thing that makes me feel happy, you know? I feel like I get so full, I — I — I just feel sick. And it's the only time that I feel good is when I feel sick like that.

SOPHIE : Have you ever thrown up?

JENNIFER : No . . .

SOPHIE : I don't believe it . . . (Jennifer laughs, then starts to cry) You *have*, you've thrown up . . . Oh no . . . Oh no . . . Oh God . . . You're so young . . . You've got to stop.

JENNIFER : I know . . . I just get so sick of food.

SOPHIE : Do you know how you're going to stop?

JENNIFER : I think I'm going to quit eating altogether. It's the only way. (She eats a forkful of cake, through her tears)

TWO INTERVIEWS: DOTTIE AND LESLIE.

DOTTIE : *I use food for every emotion that I can think of.
Including stuffing anger, which is a big one for
me. Including stuffing my own power.*

LESLIE : *I don't like the feeling of being overcommented
on. I feel like my body has been colonialized
and I resent it and I rebel against it.*

DOTTIE : *The scary world is outside of me now. I have
my food, I can just rest and be with God and go
to sleep.*

LESLIE : *I feel like I never had enough. I don't want
to say I have a food problem. I feel like I want a
lot of food, I feel like I want a lot of music, I feel
like I want a lot of feelings in my life. So I don't
have a food problem, you know? And I resent
anybody telling me that I do.*

SEVERAL WOMEN ARE GATHERED ON THE STEPS OF THE
STAIRCASE.
THE TELEPHONE RINGS AND HELENE GOES UP THE STAIRS
TO HER BEDROOM TO ANSWER IT.
NAOMI COMES OUT AND ANNOUNCES DINNER.

NAOMI : Hi, everybody . . . Everything's ready . . . The
food's out on the table in the dining room . . .

THE WOMEN GET UP TO GO INTO THE DINING ROOM.

SADIE : (To her daughter, who ignores her now)
Don't you eat a lot, Jennifer Minken . . .
(To Jackie) Help me up, now that you've
stabbed me in the back, leaving me like that.

JACKIE : I love you.

SADIE   : (Putting her arm around her) I love you, too . . .
(They walk into the dining room together)

THE DINING ROOM. PILED HIGH WITH FOOD, THE LONG
TABLE IS ENCIRCLED BY THE WOMEN, WHO START TO FILL
UP THEIR PLATES, CHATTING AND EATING AS THEY DO.

UPSTAIRS. HELENE IS IN HER BEDROOM, ON THE PHONE.

HELENE   : Where *are* you? Look, I called the Fairmont,
you are not *at* the Fairmont, you're not even
registered at the Fairmont . . . What do you
mean "fogged in?" The airplanes have
instruments, they'll land, what do you mean "fogged
in?" Where *are* you? . . . Look, Frank, I want
you to tell me the truth, you tell me exactly the
truth, what is going on here? I want to know
exactly what is going on . . . You tell me . . .
What??

THE DINING ROOM. MORE WOMEN ARE COVERING THEIR
PLATES WITH FOOD, TALKING AND LAUGHING AND EATING.

UPSTAIRS. HELENE CONTINUES ON THE PHONE.

HELENE   : Oh Frank, how could you do this to me?
How could you fucking *do* this to me? . . .
Please, Frank, please listen . . . Please come
back . . . Please *don't* . . . Don't do this, not
today . . . Frank, I love you . . . I love you . . .
Can you hear me? . . . Oh God . . . Oh . . .
Oh God . . . (It is clear he has hung up. She
hangs up phone, tries to pull herself together)

AT THE FOOT OF THE NOW-DESERTED STAIRS,
MARTINE LOOKS FURTIVELY AROUND,
THEN KNEELS DOWN TO FILM HERSELF IN THE HALL MIRROR.

AROUND THE DINING TABLE,
WOMEN ARE SITTING, EATING AND CHATTING.

THE HALLWAY. MARTINE IS FILMING HERSELF IN THE
MIRROR, ASKING HERSELF QUESTIONS AND ANSWERING
IN ENGLISH AND FRENCH.

MARTINE   :   *Pourquoi tu as fait ce documentaire?*

                Je ne sais pas . . .

                I wanted to find answers.

                Je voulais trouver les reponses . . .

                And did you find answers?

                . . .

                Est-ce que tu as encore un probleme avec la nourriture?

                Non . . .
                Non, je suis parfaitment okay, I am okay . . . .
                I feel perfectly fine . . .

                You do? . . .

                (She laughs)

                Yes, I do.

THE CAMERA PULLS BACK THE FULL LENGTH OF THE STAIRS.

EXTERIOR. NIGHT. HELENE AND NANCY OUTSIDE BY THE
POOL, LIT BY THE REFLECTION OF THE POOL-LIGHTS AND
THE MOON. THE SISTERS SIT FOR A MOMENT, SILENTLY.

NANCY : (Clears her throat) Well, honey?

HELENE : Well?

NANCY : You want to tell me what's wrong?

HELENE : He, uh, he's not coming home . . .
He's just not coming home.

NANCY : And why is that?

HELENE : That's because he doesn't *want* to come
home . . .

NANCY : Yeah, but —

HELENE : . . . That's because he's fucking tired of me . . .
That's because he's *had* it . . .

NANCY : . . . Yeah, but . . .

HELENE : . . . That's because he *hates* me, I don't know
why it is . . . I just don't know why . . . I just
don't! (She starts to cry)

INTERVIEW:
MILLIE : *My story is about starving and binging and
starving and binging. And my life is about
starving and binging . . . That's in every area . . .
With food and with money and with love . . .*

POOLSIDE. HELENE IS CRYING.

NANCY : Look, I — I — I've just got to get somebody
to be with you, honey . . . For my own reasons,
I can't deal with this right now . . . (She gets up
and exits, leaving Helene alone)

HELENE   : Oh God . . . Oh God . . . Oh please . . .

INTERVIEW:
DOTTIE   : *I would take boxes and boxes of laxatives*
                and . . . it was a progressive thing . . .
                I started out with two or three laxatives,
                then it got to 100 at one point . . .
                And I was killing myself in the past . . .
                It's a miracle I'm alive today . . .

POOLSIDE. HELENE, IS STILL CRYING, STILL ALONE.

INTERVIEW:
CORY   : *The only time I ever stopped eating was when*
                I was molested . . . I was 15, I was given a ride
                home by a businessman, I didn't think anything
                about it, and when he forced me to do some
                things, I was too scared to say no. And I didn't
                fight, I did exactly what he told, 'cause I was
                scared . . . And I stopped eating. And I got very
                thin . . . Very thin . . . And then people really
                were reacting to me differently, and I couldn't
                handle it, I just couldn't . . . I didn't — I was
                ashamed of being thin . . . I was ashamed of
                being pretty . . . and I ate again . . .

POOLSIDE. HELENE IS ALONE.
SHE HAS PULLED HERSELF TOGETHER SOMEWHAT.
KATE SLOWLY WALKS IN,
SITS DOWN ON THE ADJOINING DECK CHAIR.

KATE   : Nancy said you needed me.

HELENE   : Why did she send *you?*

KATE   : Because I'm your friend . . . What's going on?

HELENE   : I don't know. . . I feel cold . . . I feel so cold . . .

KATE   : What happened? Was it those phone calls?

HELENE   : Yeah, something to do with the phone calls . . .
             Oh Kate . . . Oh Kate . . . Oh *Kate* . . .

KATE   : What are you talking about?

HELENE   : I thought you were my friend. I *did*, I thought
             you were my friend . . . How could you do it?

KATE   : What are you *talking* about?

HELENE   : I'm talking about your affair with Frank!
             (Kate looks at her, incredulously)

THE BATHROOM.
SOPHIE IS ON HER KNEES, ON THE FLOOR,
HUNCHED OVER THE TOILET BOWL.
KATE SLAMS HER WAY IN, FURIOUS.

KATE   : What are you *doing*, Sophie? I thought you
             quit that!

SOPHIE   : Stop it, I'm sick . . . I've got the stomach flu . . .

KATE   : You are so full of shit. You're throwing up!

SOPHIE   : Will you stop it, I've got the stomach flu,
             what's the matter with you, *look* at me, I'm
             sweating and I've got a fever, can't you tell?

KATE   : I don't give a shit, that's not what I'm here for.

SOPHIE   : What *are* you here for?

KATE   : I just finished talking to Helene. She says that you told her I've been fucking Frank.

SOPHIE   : Oh, I did not.

KATE   : How could you *do* that?   You *know* that I'm not sleeping with Frank, so why would you tell Helene that I *was*? I don't get it. Just tell me *why*?

SOPHIE   : I didn't do anything . . . I *insinuated*.

KATE   : *Why*? I mean, why would you insinuate? It's not true!

SOPHIE   : Because I'm a bitch, okay? I'm a bitch and I do horrible, evil things, okay? And I don't know *why* I do them, alright?

KATE   : Women just don't treat each other like that now. What kind of a throwback are you?
I mean you're like something out of another age.
Women don't stab each other in the back.
They don't lie and they don't cheat on each other.

SOPHIE : Women aren't supposed to not invite their best friends out for lunch and not to ride their horses . . . because you invite *everybody* out to ride your horses with you, except me . . . And you and Helene *always* go out for lunch, *all* the time, the two of you, and you never invite me. *Ever* . . .

KATE : It's because you're a backstabber. It's because you do just what you did today.

SOPHIE : I don't believe you. It's because you don't like me.

KATE : Guess what? You're right. I *don't* like you.

SOPHIE : . . . I knew it . . .

KATE : I don't necessarily have to like you that much and you don't have to like me. But you *don't* mind-fuck Helene like that. Because you're her best friend. I don't get it. Why do you do it? What makes you *do* these things?

SOPHIE   : You're such a good girl, you never do anything
wrong, do you, Kate, huh, ever? I mean you
never do anything like I do. You're never a
bitch? I mean you just have *every*thing, don't
you? You've got the husband, the perfect
house, the perfect relationship, perfect sex, huh?
Everything's *perfect*, isn't it? And *I'm* the only
one, *I'm* the only one who's nasty and mean
and a bitch. And you're just *per*fect . . . Well, if
you're so perfect, why have you been going
around telling everybody today how *concerned*
you are about your *relationship*. If it's so good,
if it's so great, if it's so *perfect*, the sex is so
fabulous, and you have a *million* ways to do it,
then why are you going to ruin it, huh? You
talk about him behind his back all the time to
*every*body. Don't you think somebody's going
to tell him how unhappy you are? . . . I'm just
so jealous of you . . . I can't stand it . . . I mean,
you have every single thing I want. You have
this husband that just completely worships you
and loves you and you don't even care. You're
going to throw the whole thing away . . . It's
infuriating . . . Sometimes I just want to *choke*
you to death.

KATE   : You're creating again, Sophie. I don't talk
about him behind his back. I love him and he
knows it and everybody else knows it.

SOPHIE   : You question your marriage to *anybody*
who will listen. All you talk about very
melodramatically is how unhappy you are in
your marriage, and you don't know if it's right,
and you don't know if you want to have children.
I mean you're so fucking *boring* I can't even
believe it . . . And everybody just thinks that
you're the sweetest, most together, most sane
person here.

. . . Well, if you were so sane, you wouldn't
have to *do* this . . . I've always wanted
somebody to love me the way he loves you . . .
(Kate just stares at her disbelievingly)
Kate, please help me . . . I'm so scared . . .
I can't stop throwing up . . .
I think I'm going to die . . .

KATE   : I just don't buy it anymore, Sophie. You've
done this too many times . . . I don't care
anymore, Sophie . . . Just don't mess with my life.

SHE EXITS, SLAMMING THE BATHROOM DOOR SHUT.
SOPHIE, CRYING, TURNS BACK TO THE TOILET BOWL,
HUNCHES OVER IT, ABOUT TO THROW UP.
MARTINE'S VOICE IS HEARD OVER THE END OF THE SCENE
IN THE BATHROOM

MARTINE (V.0.) : What do you think it's about?

FINAL INTERVIEWS:

CHRIS   : *Love . . .*

CATHY   : *Survival . . .*

SADIE   : *Affection and power . . . And attention . . .*

CORY   : *It was my pal . . .*

ANITA   : *My best friend . . .*

CORY   : *It kept me safe. It kept you away if I wanted
you to be away . . .*

SADIE   : *It feels like there's life in the house . . .*
It feels like there's someone to come home to . . .
It feels like someone's coming home to you . . .
It feels like a holiday's about to happen . . .

BEA   : *I eat a lot of food because I'm pissed off.*

CATHY   : *Food for me was like a — when I think*
             about it now, it's like an angry lover, an abusive
             lover . . . and for the moment, I got off on it.
             And then afterwards I felt horrible . . .

BERRY   : *Food is control to me . . .*

LEE   : *Control . . .*

GABBY   : *Controlling my rage and controlling anxiety . . .*

LEE   : *Something inside me that can't be satisfied,*
             that always needs to be comforted and
             sedated . . .

DOTTIE   : *It's the flow of life . . .*

ANNIE   : *Daddy approval . . .*

LESLIE   : *For me, it's quite natural . . .*

ANITA   : *A silent companion, you know? . . .*

GERRI   : *It's hunger, it's satisfaction, it's comfort . . .*

GABBY   : *Protection . . .*

MARIA   : *Life . . .*

NANCY   : *Company . . .*

BERRY   : *It's everything!!*

LATER THAT NIGHT. HELENE'S BEDROOM.
HELENE AND MARTINE ARE IN THEIR NIGHTGOWNS,
SITTING TOGETHER ON A COUCH. A PLATE FULL OF
COOKIES IS ON THE STOOL IN FRONT OF THEM.

MARTINE   : Are you okay?

HELENE   : Yes . . . I really am.

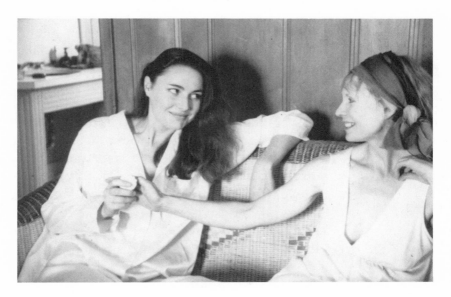

MARTINE   : What are you going to do now?

HELENE   : Ever since I was a child, I lived with others . . .
My father, my boyfriend, first husband, my
second husband . . . I don't think I've spent
three days in my life without a relationship . . .
Before I married Frank, I asked him for a
month alone, but he said no, he said he'd
waited long enough, it was now or never . . .
Well, I guess I got my wish at last. To be alone,
to see what it's like . . . It's exciting . . .
Scary, but it's exciting . . . I still have no idea
who Frank is with . . .

MARTINE   : How are you going to find out?

HELENE   : I'm not . . .

MARTINE   : I've never lived with anyone in my life, you
know . . . I mean, as an adult . . . Lately I've
been thinking, I will never be able to. 'Cause I
was stuck in myself and my problems. And I
thought I was the only person in this world
who was going through these problems. And
suddenly, a day like today, I just open up a little
bit . . . And I realized that *all* these people, *all*
these wonderful women, are going through the
same questions . . . Or *other* questions . . . But
that, you know, they're all going through *some*
questions . . . And I feel so close to them. And
it's such a *wonderful* feeling, it makes me feel, I
don't want to be alone anymore . . . I want to
be able to share things with other people, you
know? . . .
I think I'm ready now . . .
I think I don't have to be alone anymore . . .

SHE REACHES DOWN FOR A COOKIE
AS
THE SCREEN GOES BLACK.

END TITLES.

CAST

STARRING

NELLY ALARD	Martine
FRANCES BERGEN	Mrs. Williams
MARY CROSBY	Kate
MARLENA GIOVI	Sadie
MARINA GREGORY	Lydia
DAPHNA KASTNER	Jennifer
ELIZABETH KEMP	Nancy
LISA RICHARDS	Helene
GWEN WELLES	Sophie

FEATURING

TONI BASIL	Jackie
SAVANNAH SMITH BOUCHÉR	Eloise
CLAUDIA BROWN	Gabby
RACHELLE CARSON	Cathy
ANNE E. CURRY	Cory
DONNA GERMAIN	Gerri
BETH GRANT	Bea
ALOMA ICHINOSE	Maria
TARYN POWER	Anita
JACQUELIN WOOLSEY	Millie

WITH

JEANNETTE BALSIS	Jeanie
ANN BELL	Ruth
SHERRY BOUCHÉR-LYTLE	Berry
HILDY BROOKS	Molly
JUNE CHRISTOPHER	Chris
CATHERINE GENENDER	Dr. Benson
LORI HOEFT	Janice
KIM KNODE	Dottie
CLAUDIA LONOW	Lonnie
JULIETTE MARSHALL	Lee
RITA MARTINSON	Leslie
MAUREEN MCGRATH	Connie
LISE-MARIE SOBLE	Naomi
KATHERINE WALLACH	Wally
CAROLE ITA WHITE	Cece

AND

TERESA JOHNSTON

MARGOT ROSE

MINDY SEEGER

DARLENE VAN DER HOOP

PRODUCTION CREDITS

Written and Directed by	HENRY JAGLOM
Produced by	JUDITH WOLINSKY
Director of Photography	HANANIA BAER
Associate Editor	MICHELLE HART
Assistant Editor	MARY PRITCHARD
Script Supervisor	RUTH ZUCKER WALD
First Assistant Camera	MARILYN MOST DAN ELSASSER
Second Assistant Camera	DEBORAH MORGAN RANDY SHANOFSKY
Gaffer	JAMES ROSENTHAL
Best Boy/Electrician	CHRIS FENNEY
Key Grip	MARK COMBS
Grip	NEIL MONTONE
Sound Recordist	SUNNY MEYER
Boom Operator	LAURIE SELIGMAN MICHAEL RILEY
Creative Consultants	BARBARA BERCU BRUCE POSTMAN
Casting Consultant	G.M. WELLES
Costume Supervisor	CHERYL MITCHELL

Makeup   MOLLY MITCHELL

Set Decorator   ANDREA FENTON

Assistant to the Director   BRAUNA BRICKMAN

Craft Services   AMY BLANC
                                ELICIA LAPORT

"THE WAY YOU LOOK TONIGHT"

Lyrics by DOROTHY FIELDS

Music by JEROME KERN

Courtesy of PolyGram International Publishing

A JAGFILM
from
International Rainbow Pictures

ON "EATING"

ON "EATING"

by Henry Jaglom

I'm not a doctor.

I'm not a woman.

I don't have an issue of any kind with food and I don't want to come on as any kind of expert on the "subject" of this film.

Why did I make it then?

Well, I've been close to women all my life, much closer than I've been to men. I have always liked women more, always felt that I had more common ground with them. Most men, it seemed, spent their lives largely concerned with things *outside* of themselves; most women, on the other hand, dealt largely from *within* — feelings, emotions, instincts of all kinds were listened to, shared, suffered, enjoyed, explored. The great majority of men seemed determined to suppress those inner expressions, to hide them and hide from them, to deny them at all costs. Frequently they even went so far as to brutalize these threatening feelings out of existence, both in themselves and in others. They averted their eyes from those parts of themselves that frightened or embarrassed them, or that made them feel vulnerable or out-of-control, needful or scared. And what they did to one *another* was worse.

Sports and physical combat helped them initially to suppress all internal turmoil. Denial, assertiveness and aggression eventually developed to support their evasions, to affirm their look outward instead of inward. In adult life, "business" took over: Making money, gaining power, forever fighting to win battles outside of themselves became their daily routine and sustained their focus on, and interest in, the *exterior*.

Women, meanwhile, seemed free to go inside, to plunge into their *interiors*, to get to know who they were. They seemed unafraid of examining all the truly important things, as I understood them. Whether it was genetic or societal, the result was that women *felt* their feelings and *talked* about their needs and fears, their wants and anxieties. They didn't hide from themselves and they didn't hide from you, as you got to know them.

So as I developed and grew up, I came to feel that women were coping with all the important things about being alive, and I tried to open myself up with them as freely and as fully as they did with me. And I found that, quite naturally, we had much more in common than I felt was the case between me and most men. I *still* suffered certain male problems, whether inherent or conditioned: Aggression, impatience, arrogance, insensitivity and other male stupidities never were — and I'm afraid never really *are* — completely unknown or unavailable to me. But I tried, and I continue to try, to sit on the worst parts of my gender, to openly and insistently pursue an honest and unafraid look at my interior and share it in my life — and my work — with those, mostly women, who care to join me.

Now as I've said, I have long observed that as a result of the above, nothing about women and their feelings seemed alien to me. I felt deep connections and similarities between myself and the women I have gotten to know. Indeed, we seemed *so* alike in our concerns, our interests, our desires and our dreams, that I was constantly and continuously struck by the one enormous and glaring *exception* to our commonality: *Our relationship to food.*

Food is there for me. I enjoy it, I eat it and I forget about it. It has never had a meaning for me beyond that.

From my earliest encounters with women I have learned how very, very different it is with them. Each woman I've known has been, in some significant way, deeply and profoundly and undeniably *involved* with food. The manifestations have varied widely, but the issue of food and eating has existed to an astonishing degree with just about each and every one of them. Sometimes in amusing ways, frequently in touching ways, from time to time in a way so disturbing and overwhelmingly obsessive as to be truly frightening, food has come to *mean* something to most women that men simply have no idea about.

Men aren't given the message daily that their success in finding love and fulfillment revolves around the number of inches they can take off their waist or hips.

No man is told by society that his essential worth is non-existent because he doesn't look "right" in a bathing suit.

Quite simply, men don't have it hammered into them from their earliest childhood that happiness and all the good things in life can only be bought by starving themselves.

Now, I make movies.

That's what I do.

I don't exactly write and direct them in the sense that most people identify those functions. I have evolved a process by which I sort of *create* them. I make them *with* the actors and actresses who are in them. That is, I make the *raw material* that way, then I bring it back to my editing room and take the time necessary to discover what I have got, and to try to find the best way of putting it all together. I have been attacked by some and praised by others for this rather eccentric creative procedure, but I can't help myself:

That's how I do it.

A novel or a poem or a play exists in itself and stands as written. A movie doesn't exist until it *is*. A play is words on paper, *then* opens to interpretation. But the interpretation *is* the film. A movie is a smile, a tear, a look, a touch, the turn of a head, the reaction to a piece of music — all the emotions and feelings and behavior that have nothing to do with words and that cannot, should not, *must* not, be pre-determinded.

Orson Welles once said to me that the difference in the way I make movies and the way others do, was like this: "The rest of us decide what our story is going to be, and work on that, figuring we'll discover our theme *in* our story. You, Henry, decide what your *theme* is going to be and then you hammer away at *that*, figuring you'll *find* your story in it"

And, as usual, Orson got it just right.

"You're like the old Eskimo who is asked what he is making as he sits and carves an enormous walrus tusk. The Eskimo, bewildered by the question, says: 'I don't know. I'm trying to find out what's inside.' You're that old Eskimo, Henry, carving away at me, at yourself, at your friends, at your generation, carving away at your entire *culture*, trying to find out what's inside of us all . . . "

Orson got it perfectly.

When I have a theme that interests me, that seems meaningful and worth exploring, I don't write a script first thing. No, I go out and find actors and actresses who, as *people*, have concerns that are somehow relevant to the theme I'm trying to explore. And I *carve* out of them, like Orson's Old Eskimo, *their specific expressions* of what I'm attempting to look at. Then I take all those expressions back to my editing room and, for a year or two, I *"write"* my film, putting together the bits and pieces that have been given to me, making the juxtapositions, discovering the connections, creating the rhythms, until finally I have *found my story*.

Therefore, when it occurred to me that women's relationships with food were an important and unexplored aspect of the life that I saw all around me, I went out looking for women (actresses mostly, as they are skilled at expressing themselves) who — as *women* — also had a specific and unique relationship with food.

Then I created the setting, the event, the *environment* in which to let my characters loose, the superstructure (a woman giving herself a 40th birthday party) in which to *get* at the theme. And, within this design, I let the women go, encouraged and goaded and annoyed and cajoled them into as fully and freely as possible opening up in front of the camera and one another and ultimately, the audience.

And they did. And they were wonderful.

So, *that* being my way of working, it is only correct, in a book such as this, to turn the remaining pages over to as many of those women as wish to be heard. To let *them* tell you what they feel about the subject of this film. To hear *their* voices explain what *eating* means to them.

For me, finally, it has come down to this: Food, I now understand, is not what it is about. Eating, I have learned, is the *result*, not the real issue.

Food and eating, I have come to see, are a metaphor for how incredibly difficult and painful and complicated it is to be a woman in our society.

How truly *hard* it is for a woman to survive reasonably intact.

And how *triumphant* that seemingly simple act of survival really is.

Now let's hear the women speak for themselves.

ON EATING

LISA RICHARDS

HELENE

ON GETTING THE PART

My friend Gwen Welles called me and said that there was a part open in Henry Jaglom's new movie and that I should go up for it. She warned me that if Henry didn't think I had a real eating problem, he wouldn't be interested in using me in the film. "That's the way he works," she said. I walked into Henry's office. He invited me to sit down and asked me some questions about myself and my eating patterns. I said that I had been a chubby child. Henry looked at me and said that he didn't think I *had* any eating problems. Gwen's words rung out in my mind. I thought if I wanted this movie, I had better do something. I put my head down and what went through my mind was, "Oh, shit, why doesn't he think so?" I knew I didn't *seem* like someone with a problem, so when tears came into my eyes, I looked at Henry honestly and said, "I'm a *secret* eater. I don't like to talk about it." Henry said could I do that reaction on screen and would I be willing to, and I said, "Of course." That hurdle having been gotten over, Henry asked me about my life. I had just gone through a divorce and told him some of the things that had transpired between me and my husband. Henry would hear a phrase and write it down. He asked me if I minded his using it. I said no, and by the end of our conversation, he had written down several phrases and seemed to have formed a concept for a character in his mind. Before I left he said that he had never cast someone before without more knowledge of them, but that he was giving me one of the leads in the movie.

ON THE SHOOTING OF "EATING"

"Henry is difficult. Very difficult." I asked around and that's what I heard. And those words kept going through my mind. What does that mean? What *kind* of difficult? I tossed and turned through the night. Finally it was time to go to the set. Women swarmed everywhere. Upstairs in the room where we all dressed, they made little nests consisting of two chairs facing each other where they put their makeup and curlers. Turns were taken at the big mirror and little mirrors were reflecting the morning light, making patterns on the wall. Henry came up, looked at me, and said to take off my makeup, that he hated makeup. I sighed, knowing that I looked pale and bedraggled. "Oh, and don't curl your hair. I want you to look natural." I was shocked. After all, we were in Hollywood, the glamour spot of the world and Henry wants natural. Not even natural, but early-in-the-morning, just-out-of-bed realism. Others throughout the movie *did* wear makeup, but Henry was ruthless with me about that. Difficult? Well, let's say he was a director who knew what he wanted. Not having to curl my hair, I went to nibble at the large table filled with breakfast goodies in the driveway. "What are we doing first?" Nobody knows. They are setting up in the living room. I am called to come in and bring the extra dresses I had brought with me. I find out it is a scene where they are decorating for the birthday party, *my* birthday party, and Henry says to run in and see if the girls like my dress. I did and then ran off and Henry gave me another dress and sent me in again.

"More energy," was his only instruction.

In I went, not having much idea what I said. Henry catches you off-guard. He hates the planned and thought-out. He wants words that pop out of your mouth in spite of yourself, before you think. Ideas that bubble up unexpectedly and surprise. It is like being thrown into a pool, but if you go with it, it can be refreshing. Before one of my "phone calls," I asked Henry to give me five minutes to prepare because I knew it was to be an emotional scene. Henry nodded, but then in the next second, thought better of it and had me do it instantly.

"But Henry."

"Pick up the phone."

The camera is rolling. I pick up the phone. Henry says: "Your husband is never coming home again." I am stunned.

Into the phone I plead with Henry, "What am I supposed to say to that?" Henry just keeps throwing out more fuel and we get it done. Just keep swimming. If you stop and try to understand Henry's method or balk at his way, you will only get a mouthful of water. The trick is to follow Henry's direction. He has some gut level feeling of where he is going. So, yes, "difficult" he is when people try to do it only their way or produce something false or overdone. Then Henry can stop people cold and drive them to tears. But also generous. Generous in letting you try things. *Any*thing. Once Frances Bergen (who plays my mother) was being filmed talking about her children and their relationship to food. She said that her daughter never *had* a weight problem. I ran to Henry and asked to go into the scene. I told him why and he let me. I surprised Frances by saying that she never *acknowledged* my problem with food. Frances was taken aback, but she went on with the improv and we created a nice moment of conflict. Mother-daughter truth was the result. It was exhilarating, genuine, unplanned creative discovery.

ON EATING

I think of food as the mother. The good mother, the nurturing mother. I ate myself into a fat little girl. I wanted to fill the emptiness, the sense of not belonging. *My* mother was a sweet woman, a very dependent one, and not able to cope with her life. Consequently, she couldn't deal with *my* feelings of need, anger, disappointment. She wanted me to be a good little girl and I was. I didn't express my anger about my sister's birth. I ate my jealousy down and was good. That became my mode of life. Retreat from the family, in my room alone with cookies and my fantasies. Food made me feel good, but being fat was a terrible consequence. Children are extremely cruel. My parents said I was just going through a stage and that this baby fat would disappear. They kept feeding me. It kept me quiet.

When I realized the connection between food and getting fat I was about twelve and tried to starve myself. I managed to get thin. As in the movie, I *did* blow up big as a balloon when my sister was born. I *did* take an LSD trip some 20 years later and threw up for eight hours and at the end thought that I had finally "thrown up my sister." I *do* eat with my fingers. I like to nibble.

When I am happy, I eat well.

When I am anxious, I eat too much.

When I am miserable, I can't eat at all.

MARY CROSBY

KATE

I'm sitting and staring at this paper, trying to think of something witty or brilliant or profound to write.

Instead, I drop my pen and proceed to eat the *perfect* mango. It's not too cold, so I get the full flavor, lusciously juicy . . .

I now have mango juice running up to my elbows, down my T-shirt and all over this paper. I don't *have* to be witty or brilliant or profound anymore. I can simply write about the pure pleasure of a perfect mango . . .

Maybe that's why I love to eat — it's the only time my mind stops.

Making "Eating" was a joy — it allowed me to tap into all the old "stuff" and realize how good it feels that I'm not there anymore.

Unless, of course, I have a "homework" assignment to do, such as this, and there is a mango within reach.

MARINA GREGORY

LYDIA

Food Addict. That's what I am. And it's been the most difficult thing in my life to come to terms with. I'd like to lie and say that I've healed myself of this obsession with food. I haven't. I eat like a drug addict uses or an alcoholic drinks. I eat to dull the edges of what I feel. Life always seems a bit too real for me. And it's not only the *pain* of life that I seek to soften, but also the *joy*. I want to maintain an even keel, and food has allowed me to do that. It is my drug of choice. Few people understand how dangerous food can be. I've known many alcoholics who laugh when they hear the term "food addict." How can food possibly be as dangerous as drugs or alcohol?

To the point: My life revolves around food. I will plan my day around my meals. And that also means that I must have whatever specific food I've been obsessing on at the time. I've gone for months eating nothing but frozen yogurt three times a day. Frozen yogurt with yogurt chips, so that I have a mix of the soft coldness along with the crunchiness of the chips. That binge started my nails peeling and arthritis in my hands. The sugar puts me onto such a self-loathing jag that I will cancel appointments so people will not see the disgusting person I've become. I've seen friends of mine, who were trying to get off cigarettes, scrounge through the garbage for a cigarette butt to puff on. Well, I will eat around *mold* if it's the food I want and I can't get it anywhere else.

The food I obsess on, after a period of time, creates an allergic reaction. At present, that means that the frozen yogurt I eat knocks me out. First I get extremely nauseous and my body begins to ache like I'm getting the flu. And then I simply conk out. And *that*, finally, is what I've been seeking. A brief oblivion. I've been going through this routine with various foods since I was nine years old. I had no idea that this was a disease, that there were other people like me. I didn't really even think I had a problem. The weight wasn't so much of a problem for me until later, so I just thought I was weird.

It wasn't until I was asked to do "Eating" that I realized the scale of what this eating "thing" is and what an enormous amount of women suffer from it. I found a sense of sisterhood with this knowledge. But I can't say that now that I recognize my disease, I've found solace. This awareness has been a kind of hell for me over the past year of post-"Eating," because I don't yet know how to *treat* this disease. There is a lack of knowledge concerning women and food. Unless you are bulimic, anorexic or obese, people are unwilling to recognize the problem. And I even have to remind myself that I *do* have a disease and that the emotional rollercoaster I go on every day is *not* because I'm crazy, but because I don't know how to look at a plate of food without a feeling of "How do I eat this like a normal person?" hitting me in the gut. The problem is that I will *never* be able to eat like a normal person the way an alcoholic cannot have a drink like a normal person. The difference is that, as a food addict, I must *still* face food three times a day, though, for much of my life, I wished that I could completely relieve myself of that responsibility.

This movie "Eating" is very important to me because it's the first time I've seen a project that touches on the reality that food poses for so many women, including myself. I don't have a girlfriend or woman I know who hasn't gone through this in some fashion or other. What frightens me is the seeming mysteriousness of what creates this disease. Sometimes I will feel free of it, but it is always waiting. Bring up the topic of food at a table full of women and watch their eyes.

Inevitably, there will be fear.

GWEN WELLES

SOPHIE

Six o'clock this morning a woman called to tell me that she just threw up her breakfast.

Eight o'clock this morning a woman called to say she ate so much sugar that she can't go to work.

One o'clock this afternoon a woman called to tell me she just finished excercising for three hours to get rid of the dinner she ate last night.

I had so much fun helping Henry cast this film. All I had to do was look around me. Every woman I knew had *something* about food. Every single one.

Me?

None of your business.

I won't discuss *my* eating habits with *anyone.*

But I'll tell you this. Ever since playing the arch-bitch Sophie in "Eating", men have been more attracted to me than ever before.

They really have.

What do you think it means?

Excuse me.

I've got to go get something to eat.

NELLY ALARD

MARTINE

At a dinner party the other day in Paris, somebody mentions the film I did in the United States which is going to be shown the next weekend at the Deauville Film Festival, "Eating".

"What is it about?" asks the grey-haired handsome man sitting in front of me.

"Women and food," I answer, looking right into my empty plate. I know what's coming.

"Women and food?"

Around the table a few eyebrows raise in surprise.

"What *about* women and food?"

"Well, you know . . . " I mumble, "women and their own special . . . sometimes even . . . neurotic . . . relationship to food."

On my left a woman in her forties, a little plump, bursts into laughter.

"That is so *American*," she says, "women and food . . . of course *they* must have such a problem with that, *there*. Most of them are *so fat*."

"Hamburgers and Coca-Cola," says another, younger woman.

"They have such a dreadful way of eating there. Four out of five are overweight, I read."

Now it's my turn. Am I going to explain one more time that having a problem with food does not mean necessarily being fat? That the subject of "*Eating*" goes far beyond obesity??

I am not sure I have the strength to do that today.

I am not sure they will understand what I am talking about.

In Paris, whenever the word bulimia is used, it's usually by a woman saying, "I don't know what happens to me, I am completely bulimic these days . . ."; it comes with a big smile, and it means she's going to have another serving of pasta or one more piece of chocolate cake. As for throwing up deliberately . . . nobody ever *heard* of such a thing, since the Roman orgies.

So once more, I decide to talk about Jane Fonda.

Dear Jane Fonda, I want to thank you *so much* for all the situations like this, where you made me able to spread around some embarrassment and bewilderment with a wicked satisfaction. That a gorgeous creature like you couldn't help throwing up twice a day for years, suddenly shakes some of the comfortable beliefs most people here want to keep. Some years ago your story was published in several magazines here, but obviously I was the only one who read them.

But slowly things are changing.

Back home, I read in a woman's magazine a letter from a reader: a bulimic woman, asking for help. There are more and more articles about it, more and more is said about it (usually in women's magazines, not in "serious" newspapers yet). For the women concerned, the secret is still heavy.

One week later, at the Deauville Film Festival. The film raises enthusiasm. Most of the people love it. They all talk while leaving the theatre; every woman here has suddenly something to say about her own relationship to food.

"It's such a universal subject," I hear.

"There is not one woman who will not feel concerned by it."

What has happened?

So when at the press conference afterward a journalist stands up and starts saying, "How specifically *American* . . . ," I want to jump on the table and scream: "That's not true! This is *not* American, this is everywhere! Look around you!" And that *is* what I say. (Only I don't jump on the table, and I don't scream, either.)

Quietly I suggest that the *only* thing which is specifically American in this movie, perhaps, is the willingness to *talk* about the subject. And I remember what a psychiatrist told me years ago: that eating is also a substitution for talking, that a lot of people eat because they're not *able* to talk, because they don't *know* how to express their feelings.

So maybe that's the first step for us, in France, if we want to solve these problems: to stop ignoring them, and to start talking about them.

And I know it is beginning to happen.

But I will always be grateful to America and Jane Fonda for having talked about it first.

And to Henry Jaglom for making a movie about it.

FRANCES BERGEN

MRS. WILLIAMS

Eat, drink and be merry was the philosophy when I was growing up and has extended into my later years.

Today, *don't* eat too much, *don't* drink too much and be *serious* seems to be the prevailing thought.

It seems the forbiddens have proven so irresistible to so many people that they have taken them to truly frightening extremes.

So beware: Double cheeseburgers, pastries and such are only a moment on the lips, but a lifetime on the hips.

ELIZABETH KEMP

NANCY

Food. What is food? Food is ever constant. It is always on my mind. It is in my mouth all too often: w*hen, how much, how little.* It is exhausting. I would love, *truly* love, to be the person who eats whatever she wants without gaining weight. Perhaps then it would not be so important, such a compulsion. I hear people say, "Oh, I forgot to eat!" and I am devastated.

As a child, food was my pal, my comfort, my reward, my solace. As an adult, it is all of those things with one tragic addition:

It is also my punishment.

I am a prisoner of food. I seem to have two systems: One where I am in jail and one where I am out of jail.

When I am *in* jail, I am on some sort of regime; some sense of discipline, certain restrictions — it is always *very* specific. For example, I may eat two fruits, two breads, one meat, one dairy; or no fat, oil, butter, sugar or starch. I may not exceed 800 calories or 1000 calories. I have been on every known diet: The Rice Diet, The Grapefruit Diet, The TWA Diet, The Loma Linda Diet; Atkins, Stillman, Slimfast, Twinfast and Deal-A-Meal. I really work well with extremes. Once I am committed and I see results, I am immovable.

That is until I release myself from jail. Then I go on a feeding frenzy, craving sugars and breads. It is the Diet Of The Forgotten Woman. I allow myself whatever I desire, frequently in excess. I become "jolly," my laughter takes on robust tones, my breasts feel engorged and I am certain that I waddle. I am usually very funny at this time. It is exhilarating to be free. I can eat whatever I want and whenever I want, so there!

Eventually I run out of ideas of what to eat. I have ingested every craving I can think of until I have no more cravings. I go out of my way to find something, something "bad." I am slowing down. It reaches the point where it is no longer any fun. I am not funny, but morose. My body starts to thicken and out come the big shirts.

The limit has been reached and I am on my way back to jail. Thank God.

Because once I have made *that* decision I feel so much better. Being back in jail has it's advantages, after all, you see.

In jail, at least, I know I will once again have some *control!*

MARLENA GIOVI

SADIE

More, more, *more* makes for expansion, all in the wrong direction — hips, thighs, buns, etc. "Take some more, you'll feel better." Wrong!

Look, I cannot blame my eating on Mother, Father, Family or Circumstance — it's all about more for me and instant gratification. I love the Mick Jagger song, "I Can't Get No Satisfaction."

Maybe that's why he's so thin. For me, the search goes on.

What am I searching for?

I don't know. The perfect meal.

A plate of pasta with olive oil and garlic, a tossed green salad with lots of lemon. Lobster claws. Hot crusty bread. Beautiful shrimp. Fresh oily spinach. Good red wine and strong, dark espresso. Wonderful black grapes with big, hard pits.

Cannoli!

Why am I always searching for the perfect meal?

I need to find the right food to make me feel like I'm the right person.

I need the right food so I'll fit in my body.

I need the right food so I'll fit in the world.

DAPHNA KASTNER

JENNIFER

After Henry Jaglom called me in Montreal to tell me he wanted to cast me in the part of a young woman with an eating disorder, I hung up the phone, headed straight for the fridge, and gained five pounds within a week.

I had considered myself a person with relatively healthy eating habits, but for some reason my appetite suddenly became *increasingly* healthy. By the time I arrived on the set in L.A. three months later, I had gained 20 pounds. When people commented on my weight, I explained that I had gained it for a film, which was true. Only it was a lie. My weight gain *was* related to the film, but it wasn't completely intentional. It was more like a reaction. I still don't know exactly what provoked this rapid increase in food consumption. Perhaps it was my fear of the subject, perhaps nervousness at getting a job, perhaps I was just subconsciously getting into character — pulling a "Raging Bull." Whatever the reason, after a couple of days shooting, I realized that I wasn't the only one affected by the subject matter. It seemed to me that *all* the women on the set — actresses, crew and visitors alike — were running to and from the craft-service table like ants. Donuts were being hidden in purses. People were behaving strangely indeed.

But there was also something very comforting about this atmosphere. The off-camera conversation seemed to always somehow be related to food. It aroused childhood memories of being warm and safe with a bunch of mothers sitting around a picnic. It only was on the set that I realized just how profound the topic of "women and food" was. It was terribly disturbing, yet somehow extremely sensual. There were some women with whom I'd spoken throughout the shooting on the sole topic of eating. I knew *nothing* about their personal lives, but I had a strong sense of who they *were* by the way they described their relationship to food.

I play the character of a teenager who plumps herself up in retaliation to an overprotective mother whose greatest fear is that her little Jennifer will get fat. As little fat Jennifer, I'm seen throughout the movie scoffing chocolate cake in hidden corners of the house. Though I don't suffer from this eating disorder, I found that once given the license to eat as much cake as I wished, I wished to eat as much cake as I was given, and Henry finally had to keep taking it away from me between takes. Needless to say, my weight continued to escalate until the very final shot!

However, after the shooting was over, I instantly began to lose the pounds. It took about as long to lose as it did to gain, but my eating habits were now terrible. I never stopped craving the chocolate cake that I had dieted on during the filming.

RACHELLE CARSON

CATHY

As far back as I can remember, food has had a profound and traumatic effect on my life. My parents were divorced when I was almost two, and there was always a lot of anger and fighting around me from the start. I believe today that, as a child, I was lost in the crossfire. I remember feeling totally alienated and alone. Food became the solution to my overwhelming feelings very early on. In the first grade, I walked to school everyday; before school, I would stop by King's Drugstore and buy as many red hots, lemon drops and jaw breakers as my lunch money would allow. It was as if the candy was going to help me survive the events that were going to happen to me in the upcoming day.

As early as seven years old, I would be paralyzed with fear and despair. But it seemed that, if I could consume some candy or something else sweet, for that brief moment while I ate, my whole *life* would become sweet and the fear and despair would subside. Everything would be alright. Food was like a friend. It never disapproved of me or rejected me. It was something I counted on to give me pleasure and it somehow quieted the world around me.

As I grew up, it all changed. I had never had a weight problem. If anything, I was teased for being too skinny. But as I started to develop, the sugar that I had survived on was turning on me. I began to get rounder. Something in me told me that if I got fat, it was all over. What little love I felt in my life was sure to be gone. My first suicidal thoughts came around 13 or 14. The food had finally betrayed me. It stopped fixing my feelings of self-loathing, and turned into an obsession with being thin at all costs. But by this point, I was an addict. So I ate. And I threw up.

Ten years went by, trapping me in a vicious cycle of binging and starving. I was trying to gain some kind of control over my life. "If only I could stop eating," became my mantra. "If only . . . if only I could . . . if only I could stop eating," meant I would be lovable.

What I have discovered today is that I bought the lie long ago: that there was something wrong with me that needed to be fixed. I know today that food has never been my problem. How *could* it be? It is an inanimate object. *It was my lack of power.* Why couldn't I make my parents stop hating each other and love me? Or make kids at school accept me, or make my teachers approve of me? I could go on for days about why I believe I have this obsession with food. But the truth is that no one truly understands unless they have suffered the pain and humiliation of addiction themselves. I have had to work very hard to weed out all the misbeliefs and misinformation that were passed on to me from generations and generations of compulsive, addictive people who were trying to survive the only way they knew how. I was looking for love in all the wrong places. This may sound funny and even ridiculous to some, but to others it will ring true:

I was looking for love in a Three Musketeers bar.

JULIETTE MARSHALL

LEE

Food, for me, had to do with wanting to *control* something. I needed to lose weight to feel in control of my life. When I lost a certain amount of weight, I felt like I was a princess and I *owned* everything, because I'd managed to control my body, to control my feelings.

It was about *feeling*, really, you see. It was because I had needed to escape from all the feelings that I was feeling, that I started eating in the first place.

But things change.

I feel much richer in my life now than I did when I made "Eating." I have love now and I have a life. It doesn't mean that I don't have *issues* with food anymore. No, it's just that I've discovered that these issues that I thought were at the top of my list are no longer the entire sum of who I am.

I am much more than the food I eat.

Or don't eat.

And I know that now.

TARYN POWER

ANITA

Now I'm really depressed. I saw the doctor this week and weighed in at 162! *162!* Not even nine months pregnant with my third child did I weigh this much — of course when the nurse left the room, I took off the hospital gown and re-weighed myself — 160½. I took off another pound or two (after all it *was* after breakfast). Okay, 159 — give or take a few ounces. And then I checked that the scale was balanced at "0." There's no way around it — I have to face the facts. I'm gaining weight and I'm in denial.

I told the doctor that I've had an eating problem all my life, and to compound things, in the last year I gave up "carnal-animal flesh" and have consequently been eating a lot of starches and pasta. He agreed that I had a "carb" body. He said he could tell the moment I walked in. I've gained 20 pounds since I last saw him two years ago. I felt miserable, embarrassed, ashamed. I cried.

I briefed him on my eating history and asked him if he'd ever heard of Limits — *that* had been my first exposure to dieting. This was back in 1962. My family and I were living in Rome, Italy, and noticing my "butter-ball" (my nickname at the time) figure, my mother took me to the doctor. (I had felt then, and still do now, that there was a lot of shame and embarrassment felt on her part because of my rotund body.) Dr. Stallone put me on two Limits cookies (cheese or chocolate flavor) and a glass of milk per meal, and I was on my way. So while my family sat down at mealtime in our beautiful villa on the Appian Way, and savored *risotto alla milanese* and *gnocchi alla romana*, I stared down at my unassuming Limits cookies (at least they had cream fillings).

But you see, this was all *after* the fact. For the facts succeed the feelings and the feelings are often harder to locate and identify. My early childhood is in fact one big confusion, and not until my old English nanny resurfaced last year and began to shed light on the picture, did I have *any* idea how, where and with whom I spent my early years.

I do recall hiding behind the barcounter in my grandmother's home in Mexico City (my sister and I had been sent to live there with her after my father's death in 1958) and devouring strips of fresh, raw, salty bacon; anxiously waiting for the "tortilla lady" to make her entrance through the garden gate, so I could get my share of the soft, aromatic, warm Mexican staple with melted butter and salt; pillaging the sumptuous birthday cakes before the lavish parties.

And I recall a lot of sadness — sadness and loneliness. A deep, disorienting loneliness.

Food became my buddy. I'd steal it — hide with it — lie for it — long for it — and it was the end-all — the pot of gold at the end of the rainbow — the honored guest at any table — my silent companion.

I found great comfort in food and in the company of cooks — the large Mexican and Italian mamas always at work in the kitchen over the hot stoves preparing some delicacy. Their largeness, warmth and kindness crept under my skin and into my heart and transformed my outlook and priorities in life. I conjured to be like them — a nurturing "mama." To date I am a mother of three. I still have not made it as a *mama*, and I can't hack it as an actress. I'm told I have the face of a leading lady and the body of a character actress. So I hang in and we all hang out at home.

At 13 I came by some diet pills and diuretics. By 14 I was prescribed a thyroid extract in hopes that *that* might aid my

metabolism. Then, at 15, I learned about *calories*. I finally stopped
sucking my thumb, lowered my caloric intake, increased my output
(standing in shirt sleeves outside in the Swiss Alps in winter to "burn"
them off) and I began to lose . . . and lose . . . and lose. And the
more I lost, the less I took in and the more I put out. I had finally
found the formula!

For years I had suffered the abuse of being teased. Now I
vowed that my family would end up having to visit me as I lay on
my deathbed — skinny at last, in the *hospital*.

When my mother finally suggested I looked green and
emaciated, I knew I had finally reached my goal!

I developed anorexia, soon followed by bulimia. In those
days I was unaware they had names. I just didn't want *anything* in
my body. I was going to be skinny, stay skinny, go *beyond* skinny.

I put myself on a coffee diet. I lived on caffeine and fresh
air.

I took up "pot," but it gave me the "munchies" too often. So
I took up alcohol, but found out it was laden with calories. I started
a program: green salad one night, fruit salad the next, gin and Coca-
Cola the third. It worked for a season.

I tried macrobiotics.

I tried vegetarianism.

I tried this. I tried that.

And my weight rose and fell. Yet even at my lowest weight,
I still "felt" fat. When I'd shed the weight, I'd feel like I was losing
my *self* — like I was disappearing, like I didn't exist. I had trouble
identifying with my slim self. I still do.

And the camera knew. My acting career suffered. "She
needs to lose weight," was the incessant feedback. I got exasper-
ated. Discouraged. Depressed. I would never succeed, never make
it in my chosen career. They couldn't see past my body.

Then I get a break — I bump into Henry Jaglom at a late night
Hollywood deli. He tells me he's preparing a movie and asks me
if I have any "eating problems." My mouth falls open. I can't believe
it. We speak briefly, then later in his office for a long time.

I got the job.

I join a radical Overeaters Anonymous group called *"How."*
I am ecstatic when I find out I have lost 18 pounds in 30 days.

I want to look perfect on camera.

But production on the picture keeps being postponed and I have trouble maintaining my low weight. I start to gain back a few pounds. Then a few more. I feel defeated, miserable, lost. My weight is spiraling back up. But wait a minute! That's what this movie is going to be *about* anyway, isn't it?

Finally, an acting part I totally qualify for.

At last, a movie I *can't* have the "wrong weight" for.

I am ready.

LORI HOEFT

JANICE

I *think* I'm healthy about it, but people will actually come up to me sometimes and say things like, "If you would lose 30 pounds, you could have anything." And then I wonder if I should go to the gym to try to lose 30 pounds so I can have anything.

KIM KNODE

DOTTIE

I must live to eat — I mean I must eat to live — yet my manner of living and eating has begged for sanity.

Memories of childhood in Tokyo as the middle child of an affluent father in business and a glamorous stepmother are filled with sugar. The fancy cakes, the cookies, the maids, the chauffeurs, my teachers, my home — they all pointed toward a perfect picture. Yet I chose to fill an emotional hole with food. I didn't know how to express with words, simple statements such as:

"I feel abandoned because mommy left for another man."

"Daddy, why don't you hug me more?"

"Step-mommy, why are you pretending to love me when I know you love my little brother more?"

I flew away from home after high school, but when I got to the States I was overwhelmed by the size of American supermarkets. Culture shock was suppressed in college by deprivation.

I starved myself down to 89 pounds.

I was driven to desperation and started looking for help. I have tried countless diets, spiritual counselors and shrinks. After years of bouncing back and forth in my weight and in my attitudes and my attractions for various men, I have discovered some hidden treasures in all my experiences.

Loving acceptance of myself always works.

Praying to God for guidance always works.

Results of supplications to a Supreme Being may not instantaneously appear, but sooner or later I have proof God has healed with His majestic hand.

Men, food and money still sway me, yet I have found a piece of my heart which can only be mine.

CATHERINE GENENDER

DR. BENSON

I basically replaced love with food. Everyday eating, putting food in my mouth and saying, "You can't be this bad, if you were, who would give you a box of Godiva chocolates?"

ANNE E. CURRY

CORY

A vivid childhood memory: getting caught with overstuffed cheeks long after mealtime and suffering through the humiliation of emptying them into my mother's hand. When she thought I was hiding more, she'd reach inside my mouth and I can still feel her nails dragging against the inside of my cheeks. "What have you *got* in there?", she'd say, disbelievingly.

Recently, I returned to my parent's home and I found this old photo album. I opened up the album and I was going through it, and there was this picture of this little girl, after her birthday party, sitting alone at the end of a long table. Nobody else was in the room. And she had gone around the table, and she had collected *all* of the cake that everybody *else* had left on their plates. And she was sitting at the end of the table with this little party hat on and in this little party dress, she was sitting with all the leftover cakes, and she was eating all the other children's leftover cakes.

Years later, I had become the perfect hostess. Everyone said so. I would always insist on clearing the dinner table by myself. No thanks, I don't need any help. You go out and enjoy the company.

I'll clean up in here.

Once in the kitchen, alone with all the leftover plates, my insatiability would have its way. Nobody knew that the *reason* I was such a perfect hostess was so that I could eat every single thing that my guests had left behind on each and every one of their plates.

Food for me, you see, is a skull and crossbones.

It always will be.

Next time you meet a perfect hostess, follow her into the kitchen.

JUNE CHRISTOPHER

CHRIS

My grandmother was 350 pounds. She used to jiggle when she walked, which, of course, grossed us all out. My mother is fanatically skinny. Food has always been a big subject all my life; I used to have a lot of problems with it. I think I confused love with food — meaning that I had to be skinny to get love and that I had to look perfect in order to be loved. I got to the point in my growth, where I realized that the fact that I didn't love *myself* was the reason why I wasn't getting love, not because I wasn't perfect looking. But it took a long time for me to *get* that. And now that I've *got* that, I feel I can get anything.

SAVANNAH SMITH BOUCHÉR

ELOISE

All my life I have lived with a kind of loneliness that I thought was hunger. I never suspected I was lonely, because I lived in a house full of family who loved each other to distraction. But that still wasn't enough for me. Nothing was ever enough, even though Daddy read "Uncle Remus" at night to my sister Sherry and me until we fell asleep. And Mother made our matching moonbeam costumes by hand for when we danced at the tap and ballet recital.

Still nothing was ever enough.

So I always felt lonely for something or someone and I thought it was my stomach that was empty. And to make things better I would feed myself. It was usually against my parent's wishes, because they wanted me to be slim and pretty, so I developed a kind of *shame* around my behavior. I would *sneak* and eat wherever and whenever I could, thinking I was getting what I wanted to ease the pain of what I thought was my hunger. But all I got was *full* for awhile, and then I would quickly become hungry again. And it began again.

So started the endless ups and downs of *do* I eat or do I not

eat or shall I fast and take colonics? Maybe I will have only fruit.
I'll eat everything I want for three days and then not eat for a week.
I'll do the Pregnant Woman's Urine Shot Diet again or I'll go back
to Jenny Craig. But the Diet Center is safer and if only I was in love,
I wouldn't be hungry.

For a while.

But when we fight and break up, I'm really not hungry
because I'm so lonely.

But there's nothing I'd rather do when I'm alone than to feel
full and escape the feeling of emptiness.

I don't know. Maybe it's me. I've been lonely for all my life.
I don't know how to love myself, but I *do* know how to feed me.

No matter how much it hurts.

SHERRY BOUCHER-LYTLE

BERRY

As a child I was very skinny. I had no tits. And all of a sudden I woke up one day and I looked down and I thought, "You know if I'd eat more maybe it would stop *here.*" Like the food would just come right down to my neck and just stop *here.* And people might pay more attention to me. So I ate. And I got a figure. When I was 13, I won a pageant, just on my body, and I said, "Wow, I'm going to eat more gumbo, more okra and more *everything* and then people are really going to look at me."

But mother never told me that banana puddin', chicken and dumplings, black-eyed peas and corn bread, those warm and gloriously delicious Southern foods, would ruin me for life. I was going along, happily eating everything in sight, when *Twiggy* happened. I was 21 and nice and round and suddenly *thinness* was all anybody talked about. Thin is beautiful. You can never be too thin. Look like a boy and everyone will love you.

There was just one problem. It was too late. Thin didn't *feel* good. Being *heavier* seemed to comfort me, like a wool blanket on a snowy morning. Eating now meant stuffing cotton candy down my emotional hole and trying to fill it up so the pain and anger would go away.

What pain and anger?

At what?

I'm not sure.

But I think it was at not being thin!

DONNA GERMAIN

GERRI

I like to eat. I really like it. I have such a big appetite and I like all kinds of foods. I wasn't the kind of child who didn't like certain things. I even liked *liver*. And then what happened to me, when I was an adolescent, was that I really got brainwashed. I mean really good. I started to wear used clothing once I started to develop a real body, and I started to get round. I wanted to be thin. I only weighed 116 pounds, but that wasn't thin enough.

And so I started this thing that I did for 15 years of constantly eating and eating and not enjoying any of it and then going on these liquid-protein diets. Do you want to know what liquid protein is? It's this kind of glue-like substance that tastes like cowhide. And I would live on it for two or three weeks at a time. And then I'd start eating again. Back and forth. Endless. 15 years!

But you know what I think now?

I think that I should think less about *my* food problems and just be grateful that I've got enough to eat every day. And maybe I could spend some of this energy and time trying to help create a world where everybody else can finally have enough to eat.

BETH GRANT

BEA

The loss of my grandfather and his unconditional love had a direct connection to my eating problems. I went to the sugar he taught me to love as a substitute for him. Desperately addicted to sugar, I've always had a love-hate relationship with food. By the time of my doing this film, I had given sugar up altogether in an effort to find some sanity in my eating. But I was still suffering a daily battle with the obsession to eat *over* my feelings, to eat *over* good news, bad news, life . . .

I was jogging one morning before work and a sudden rage came pouring out of me: A rage at *men* I had tried to rise above, a rage for all the times I was rejected for a more attractive, *thin* woman, a rage at all the times I felt *less* than, all the times I was considered second-best, all the hurt and pain that had taught me to hate my body, hate my precious self, because I wasn't built according to someone else's standards. I ran and I raged and I arrived on the "Eating" set with a vengeance, ready to find a vehicle for all these feelings. Making the movie became a catharsis for me. I liked it. It felt good. But I couldn't wait for it to end.

ALOMA ICHINOSE

MARIA

   While the rest of the girls were waving their pom-poms, listening to rock-and-roll and dreaming of their very own rebel, "Maria" couldn't stop thinking about Chanel's ankles. Her dream was a simple one, lifted from the endless hours of flipping through *Photoplay* and *Vogue* at the Las Palmas Newsstand. It was there that *Audrey, Ava* and *Coco* came to life. They were the whippets of fashion and film with the stats to prove it: 34-24-34. But it wasn't really those particular numbers that "Maria" was worried about; she already had those. It was her ankles. Compared to the rest of her, her ankles looked like imports from the fields of Russia.

   With Saran Wrap now being sold at all the supermarkets, her destiny became obvious to her. Instead of ankles that made her feel like a peasant, there was hope for those rich-lady ankles that never walked anywhere practical. The ones shaped for tea parties and summers in the Hamptons. Could she beat the odds?

   At night, she would wrap and wrap, pulling wool socks over the enemies. Alone, in the privacy of her small bedroom she would stretch the clear Saran Wrap bandages around each ankle 20 times.

So what if she had to sleep with her legs propped up on the pillow? That seemed a rather small sacrifice. The idea occurred to her that she should be wearing the bondage gear full time, to increase sweat and reduction, of course. School and dating interfered with her plan for total Saran Wrap surrender, although she *did* try it a few times.

The Saran Wrap phase lasted about a year. Her ankles held out longer. The truth is that she stopped thinking about them. Other obsessions came and went. Presently, "Maria," 40-plus, can be found at Safeway searching the shelves for a product to save her mind.

TONY BASIL

JACKIE

The first dreams that I recall in the crib were about food. Food in the crib. Then after I got *out* of the crib, I used to take food into *bed* with me. My mother used to catch me taking bread into bed with me.

Thank God, I don't have any problem with food anymore. Not at all.

Just as long as I don't keep any in the house.

CAROLE ITA WHITE

CECE

It is said that life cannot tolerate a vacuum. Neither can I. So when there are no men in my life, I fill that vacuum with food. "Fill" is the operative word here. See, I crave the sensation of feeling filled.

It's that hugged feeling. That body to body, flesh to flesh thing.

FILL, FILLED, FULL.

When that feeling is not to be had by any direct means, there is another way to go: FOOD.

It is in the eating stage of consumption that food most closely duplicates the human connection.

It's the lifting of the warm, moist Mrs. Fields Oatmeal-Raisin cookie to the lips . . . the chewing . . . the savoring . . .

It's that shiver you feel when you taste your first lick of chocolate-raspberry truffle ice cream . . .

And who can forget the heat of the perfect salsa on the palate? Burning, desperate to be quenched . . .

So maybe now you're thinking "Why bother with men at all?"

Dating is so hit and miss. The divorce rate is so high.

Here is why.

Men will come. Men will go.

BUT FOOD STICKS AROUND!

Around your stomach, your behind and your thighs.

And please don't forget your arteries.

As children we cry for our mother's embrace and what are we given? A bottle of milk and a zwieback cracker. Food soon becomes an acceptable substitute for the human touch.

Well forget it. Not *this* baby! Food is the wolf in sheep's clothing, and the first one is always free.

I say men may not be perfect, but give me heartbreak over heart attack any day.

LISA-MARIE SOBLE

NAOMI

   I used to sneak bread when I was little. I used to eat the *whole* loaf of bread. I'd throw out the white part and I'd eat all the crust and I'd put butter on it. And I still do that in times of tension. Except I don't eat the butter anymore . . .

   You know what I do *now* to keep from eating? I fool myself. I make a huge pot of very strong English tea and I drink it with lots of low-fat milk and lots of *Equal* and I fool myself into thinking that I'm having a great treat. I have maybe *eight* cups a day, on an average, so that I won't miss eating other things. Every night is still a problem, though. I lay in bed at night on my back and I sort of hold onto my hip bones. And if they don't stick out enough, if they don't protrude the way I'd like them to, if the *hollow* isn't there, you know, or isn't hollow *enough*, then I know I've eaten too much that day. And so I have to be extremely careful the next day. And drink even *more* pots of tea with even more low-fat milk.

   And *Equal* by the carton.

MAUREEN MCGRATH

CONNIE

I resent food because I need it, because I need to *eat* it. And I don't like to *need* anything . . .

My mother never ate. I didn't have a father. And when my mother ate, she ate like half a tomato and a little hamburger patty and she was full.

But she's perfect.

JEANETTE BALSIS

JEANIE

   I think it was the pressure that I had to look perfect, to always be perfect, to always live up to the perfection of the rest of my family. When I grew up and got a boyfriend and fell in love, I couldn't eat anything because I wanted to look perfect. And when he left me, I felt like, "Well, he left me because I'm too fat!" So I tried to starve myself, I binged, and then I would throw up. And when I finally broke up with him, I just knew that it was because I just wasn't good enough. Because I was too fat.

JACQUELIN WOOLSEY

MILLIE

Henry Jaglom just called and asked me where my contribution was to this book. He reminded me that I promised to bring it in several weeks ago. I started laughing and told him I hadn't been able to get to it — or anything else — because I've just been on a two-week *binge*.

Last Sunday I found myself at Winchell's Donuts stuffing down an apple fritter, four or five assorted donuts, and going from there to have dinner, topping it off with chocolate-chip cheesecake, then stopping to buy pecan pie on the way home — trying, just *trying* to get the secure feeling I used to get on Saturday mornings when my mother brought home hot, fresh, baked glazed donuts from the bakery for us all to eat, and I would feel safe and loved at last.

Moderation is just a rumor in my life. I've been educated beyond my ability to learn: I've been Therapized, Analyzed, Rolfed, Rebirthed, Neo-Reiched. I've been in recovery for every compulsive obsession known to woman, except gambling. I'm in the most active religion in the world and I chant constantly, and believe me *all* of these things have sustained and nurtured me and have saved my life.

But sometimes, like Elvis, I still want donuts to fix it all. And they don't. Please take my word f~ ``

HENRY JAGLOM'S FILMOGRAPHY

FiLMOGRAPHY

1968   Actor: <u>PSYCH-OUT</u>, directed by Richard Rush. (A.I.P).

1969   Actor: <u>THE THOUSAND PLANE RAID</u>, directed by Boris Sagal. (Oakmont/United Artists).

1969   Editorial Consultant: <u>EASY RIDER</u>, directed by Dennis Hopper. (BBS/Columbia Pictures).

1970   Actor: <u>THE LAST MOVIE</u>, directed by Dennis Hopper. (Universal).

1971   Writer, Director: <u>A SAFE PLACE</u>, starring Tuesday Weld, Orson Welles and Jack Nicholson. Introducing Gwen Welles. With Philip Proctor. (BBS/Columbia Pictures).

1972   Actor: <u>DRIVE, HE SAID</u>, directed by Jack Nicholson. (BBS/Columbia Pictures).

1973   Actor: <u>LILY AIME-MOI</u>, directed by Maurice Dugowson. (Camera One, Paris).

1973   Actor: <u>THE OTHER SIDE OF THE WIND</u>, directed by Orson Welles. (Unreleased).

1974   Presenter: <u>HEARTS AND MINDS</u>, directed by Peter Davis. (BBS/Rainbow Pictures/Warner Bros.). Academy Award: Best Documentary Feature.

1976   Writer, Director: <u>TRACKS</u>, starring Dennis Hopper, Taryn Power, Dean Stockwell. Introducing Michael Emil and Zack Norman. With Topo Swope, Alfred Ryder, Barbara Flood, Richard Romanus. (International Rainbow Pictures).

1980   Writer, Director, Actor: <u>SITTING DUCKS</u>, starring Michael Emil and Zack Norman. Introducing Patrice Townsend. With Richard Romanus, Irene Forrest and Henry Jaglom. (International Rainbow Pictures/United Film Distribution).

1982   Director: THE MUNICIPALIANS (segment of NATIONAL LAMPOON'S MOVIE MADNESS), starring Robby Benson, Richard Widmark, Elisha Cook, Jr., and Christopher Lloyd. (United Artists).

1983   Writer, Director: CAN SHE BAKE A CHERRY PIE?, starring Karen Black and Michael Emil. With Michael Margotta, Frances Fisher, Martin Harvey Friedberg. (I.R.P./Castle Hill).

1985   Writer, Director, Actor: ALWAYS *(BUT NOT FOREVER)*, starring Henry Jaglom and Patrice Townsend. With Alan Rachins, Joanna Frank, Melissa Leo, Bob Rafelson, Jonathan Kaufer, Andre Gregory, Michael Emil, Amnon Meskin, Bud Townsend, Peter Rafelson. (I.R.P./Jagfilms/Samuel Goldwyn Co.).

1987   Writer, Director, Actor: SOMEONE TO LOVE, starring Orson Welles, Sally Kellerman, Michael Emil, Andrea Marcovicci, Oja Kodar and Henry Jaglom. With Dave Frishberg, Ronee Blakley, Stephen Bishop, Kathryn Harrold, Monte Hellman, Barbara Flood. (I.R.P./Jagfilms/Castle Hill).

1989   Writer, Director, Actor: NEWS YEAR DAY, Introducing Maggie Jakobson. Co-starring Henry Jaglom and Gwen Welles. With David Duchovny, Milos Forman, Harvey Miller, Irene Moore, James DePreist, Michael Emil. (I.R.P./Jagfilms).

1990   Writer, Director: EATING, starring Mary Crosby, Frances Bergen, Gwen Welles, Lisa Richards. Introducing Nelly Alard. With Marlena Giovi, Daphna Kastner, Marina Gregory, Elizabeth Kemp, Beth Grant. (I.R.P./Jagfilms).

1991   Writer, Director, Actor: VENICE/VENICE, starring Nelly Alard and Henry Jaglom. With Suzanne Bertish, Daphna Kastner, Melissa Leo, David Duchovny, Suzanne Lanza, Diane Salinger, Simon Callow, Marshall Barer, Zack Norman, Lisa Richards, Elizabeth Kemp and John Landis. (I.R.P./Jagfilms).

1992   Writer, Director: LUCKY DUCKS, starring Michael Emil and Zack Norman. With Gwen Welles, Donna Germain, Richard Romanus, Casey Siemaszko, Daphna Kastner, Frances Fisher, Roscoe Lee Browne, Noel Harrison, Harry Nillson, Sandy Baron, George Furth, Harvey Miller, Richard Perry. (I.R.P./Jagfilms).